I0665933

REFLECTIONS FROM THE OTHER SIDE

REFLECTIONS
FROM THE
OTHER SIDE

JC MOWREY

This book is a work of fiction. Names, characters, places and incidents either are products of the author's imagination or are used fictitiously. Any resemblance to actual events or locales or persons, living or dead, is entirely coincidental.

Copyright © 2025 by JC Mowrey
Edited by Dylan Garity
Cover and interior design by Daniel Pyle

ISBN: 979-8-9934817-0-8

All rights reserved. This book or any portion thereof may not be reproduced or used in any manner whatsoever without the express written permission of the publisher except in the case of brief quotations embodied in a book review.

To Sam, Jacob, and Erin. You showed me that I could choose how I wanted my life to be.

FOREWORD

I have never once expected or hoped that a person would hear my story and feel any amount of sympathy for me. I've hidden so much of my past because I am certain that anyone who saw the entirety would be appalled by me and my actions. I accept who I am, and I will not make apologies for it.

People don't watch the horrors of the world with compassion at the forefront of their mind. They watch as the worst of mankind commits atrocity after atrocity, and the prevailing question is always the same. Why? Why do people do what they do? Why do people feel the compulsion to harm, maim, and kill? It's the reason we are so fascinated with documentaries and biopics about the horrors of our lifetime. Humans have an insatiable desire to analyze and understand the cause of these things.

I know it would be more comfortable if I had been following some noble cause that led me down this path.

People could relate and feel safer thinking that I stalked and dispatched other criminals when justice failed. I'm sure it would even be nice if my actions were motivated by vengeance, profit, or deep existential beliefs, but that is not close to the truth.

People constantly feel the need to lie to themselves and those around them, in the naïve hope of making life more bearable. The conundrum is how capable a person is of enjoying reality and existence if they must lie to themselves or others. True happiness stems from genuine expression of the self. My preferred method of genuine self-expression happens to be hostile and dangerous to others.

I have seen what happens when people are stripped of the masks they wear for others' sakes and show their true faces. I ceased believing there was purpose in observing social mores as I noticed the foundation of society was fickle and bound to crumble. Have you ever watched a mother throw her own child onto the butcher's table in a selfish attempt at self-preservation? I have, and it was beautiful. That one singular moment, witnessing the selfishness and brutality of human existence. Parents, spouses, friends, and the rest, all reduced to quivering cowards as they near death. I wish I would have let those people live, so they could be haunted by the visions of what I did and know that it was their fault. That would have been a fate far worse than death.

I have experienced many different aspects of humanity throughout my life and, never once, did any of it deter me from the path I walked. I don't know why I'm different than others. I only know my reasons for my actions, and that reason is extremely simple. The truth is that my reason is you. My reason is the people I encounter on a daily basis and the disgust I have for each and every one of them.

1

I was raised in a small town in Kentucky in a middle-class family. I had two sisters, a mother, and a father. Our house was in a decent and nondescript neighborhood. There was minimal crime, aside from the occasional drug use by a rebellious teenager. On the surface, I would assume my environment mirrored what people refer to as the "American dream."

Some of this will be difficult to admit. I have spent decades wearing a mask to better fit in with those around me. What I have just described is the surface of my childhood. For much of my life, I would've honestly described my early years as being normal and without trauma. Yet that was ignorance, bred from a lack of exposure to the experiences of those who are better adjusted.

My family could perhaps be best defined as hostile. I didn't realize it much at first, because our interactions were the norm for me. However, I started to realize how broken our family unit was when I was eight years old. None of us were close with each other. My oldest sister was born several years before me. By the time I fully realized how destructive and caustic my family was, she was disenchanted with them and did her best to stay away as much as possible. My other sister is right between us in age, and like any middle child I've met, she struggled with self-image. She hated herself more than anyone, and as a result was incapable of interacting kindly with the rest of us.

My parents' marriage was one of convenience and religious obligation. They hated each other, but divorce would have been irresponsible—and worse, a sin. The majority of their interactions consisted of silence and feigned tolerance.

This anger and resentment leaked into how they bonded with us children. My father would shut down on a daily basis, choosing to escape his misery with television or alcohol. We never once had a meaningful conversation during my early childhood. He wasn't abusive or aggressive with me, he was merely absent. My mother, on the other hand would take out her anger on us verbally. My sisters were bombarded with criticism of their clothing, their sexual promiscuity, or any other aspect of themselves my mother could sink her fangs into.

I received a different form of criticism. I was not told how wrong my decisions were. I was never yelled at for not completing chores. No, I was belittled for the simple fact that I was born a male. Before I was even ten years old, my mother told me countless times how incompetent and useless men were. According to her, we were all heartless and moronic perverts who wouldn't know how to be helpful if we were given an audio instruction book with accompanying photos. I remember sitting next to her while she spoke with friends about her current menstrual cycle and the mood swings associated with it. I was completely ignorant to them, but I remember recognizing that she would describe her outbursts of anger as PMS. I asked curiously what that was, and my mother looked directly into my eyes and told me, "Putting up with Men's Stupidity." I was seven at the time.

She was a hyper-critical and overbearing monster that I tolerated as much as I could. However, I never let her disdain for me alter how I saw myself. I was an extremely high-achieving child. I never once received below an A in school, and I was a fairly well- rounded athlete starting from the age of six. My family never truly recognized, praised, or rewarded me for my accomplishments. Yet I never interpreted that as my family hating me. They were just busy with their own lives. I even understand that my mother's disdain for men was not a reflection of her interactions with me.

The only time we, as a family unit, were polite and cordial was when we were in public. When strangers could peer into the keyhole of our connections, everyone was expected to act like we loved each other. There was to be nothing but support and care, for the sake of appearances.

This confused my concept of love from a very early age. These interactions in public accomplished two separate tasks: The first was to teach me that love was an action that you performed for the sake of ensuring people didn't get too close. If there is ever a risk of exposure, shower the risk in feigned compassion and niceties until they cease their questioning and accept the version of you that you want. Second, it taught me the importance of manipulation. These social outings acted as the first strips of glue-covered newspaper that would eventually form the mask that I used to escape suspicion and detection by law enforcement.

These interactions in my early years laid the foundation for my understanding that I didn't belong. I was different somehow. I never fit in with my own family, which caused difficulty in understanding social interactions as I started into daycare and then elementary school. These difficulties interacting with peers further entrenched the idea that I didn't fit in with the bulk of society.

Surviving at home was actually a fairly easy task. The first rule for survival was to ingratiate yourself to the rest of the family. Even if it's a complete lie, compliment and show gratitude for every small amount of effort that someone else might have accidentally exerted. This allowed them to see me as a "good" kid and ignore me, for the most part. And being ignored was always the superior option.

The second rule for survival was to ensure that you completed every task to completion. Given a chore? Go above and beyond what would be expected of the most stringent and OCD veteran. I learned very young that my mother would purposely set small traps to ensure she could yell at me and my sisters for being lazy. She would leave a scrap of paper underneath a large lamp when we were supposed to dust. She would purposely leave a hair across the buttons of the television so she could see if we dared watch any shows when we should have been cleaning. By the age of eight, I learned the rules and became proficient in adhering to them. My middle sister would often shirk the chores or take short-cuts, landing her in more trouble.

The third rule, and possibly the most important, was to be neither seen nor heard as much as possible. I learned quickly to sneak through the house like prey in unfamiliar territory, or like a predator stalking that very same prey. If you were unseen and unheard, you couldn't be challenged in any way.

I created a fourth rule, my own rule: take the enemy by surprise. The traps weren't just set for chores; my parents would often intentionally set them in conversation, looking to find further reasons to be angry. Neither of my sisters developed this fourth rule, and they struggled more often with our wardens. The greatest tool at my disposal was honesty. My parents would ask questions while already knowing the truth, and would be so convinced that I would lie when answering, ready to spring the trap, that when I was 100 percent honest, they never knew how to respond. I still chuckle thinking of the shocked and frozen looks on their faces when I told them at twelve that a pack of cigarettes was mine because I smoked daily and had stolen it from a teacher's purse. They were so taken aback by that one that they never actually punished me for it.

Whether they were hostile or absent, the role they played was never a positive one. Yet even with all of this, I do not despise my family. They are simply who they are. I do not hate the sloth for being slow, nor the lion for eating the gazelle. That hatred would be just as pointless and confusing. I am apathetic toward them. I do not owe my parents any kindness or gratitude for giving birth to me (especially as it wasn't intentional and was heavily regretted, as they informed me on more than one occasion). I see no obligatory connection between my sisters and me simply because we share some DNA. They just happened to be the people who occupied the same living space as me while I was growing. Nothing more, nothing less.

My family was often absorbed in their own worlds, and so starting when I was nine, during the summers, I was regularly told to leave the house and "be a kid" outside. This was a difficult chore for me, though. I had no real friends in the neighborhood and had never had much of an interest in making any. More friends meant more people in my life, and that directly translated to more irritation at having to maintain appearances. I would often just walk the neighborhood for hours, possibly stop at a gas station and buy a snack with the meager money I was able to find while completing my chores.

I did eventually start spending time with a girl in my neighborhood. She was six years older and lived two streets over. On days when it was particularly humid or my ginger skin was beginning to show the early signs of an oncoming sunburn, she would let me come into her house for a brief reprieve from the sun. I never considered her a friend, per se. She was merely an acquaintance maintained for convenience. She actually taught me several important lessons about people.

One day, while I was walking through the neighborhood, she was sitting outside and called out to me. She said that she noticed I looked warm and offered me some water.

Moving forward, I would stop by her house on occasion for the break and we would share small talk. She was always alone at home because her parents had to work during the day. She was polite enough, but I never really understood why she was being so nice to me. There didn't seem to be any ulterior motives or hidden agendas.

One day, when I stopped by, her door was unlocked but she didn't respond when I knocked. I opened the door and let myself in because politeness was not the priority while I stood baking in the heat. I went to the kitchen and helped myself to a glass of water, and then I heard a voice coming from her bedroom. I didn't understand it at the time, but later I discovered that the scene I walked in on was her performing oral sex on some older boy I didn't recognize. Upon seeing me, he yelled at me, and she looked horribly embarrassed. I left the room and returned to the kitchen to finish my water.

Eventually, she and the boy came out and he left,

shooting me a cruel stare on his way. She apologized, which I thought was odd considering it was her house. I later learned that she was actually selling sexual favors to some of the teenage boys and some of the adult men in our area. I do not judge her for her money-making endeavors. Once I fully understood what she was doing, I actually respected her ability to use what she had at her disposal to thrive. She didn't come from a very supportive household and she made do.

I remember one time when she was allowing me to spend time in her living room because it was a particularly scalding day. It was just her and me in the house. She offered me a beer to cool off from the heat, which I graciously accepted. As I drank the forty of Mickey's and listened to whatever music she'd put on, I saw her just casually looking at me. Her stare didn't bother me in the least, but it did confuse me.

I looked over at her and asked, "Is something wrong? Do I need to leave?"

She sat there in her cut-off Daisy Duke shorts and bright red tube top. Her pink and black hair was cut to her shoulders, but on this day, she was keeping it in a ponytail. "No, you don't need to go anywhere. But I do have a question for you, if it's cool."

"Yeah. What's up?" I asked curiously. She rarely asked me anything. She would talk about herself at times and occasionally offer me beer or cigarettes while telling me about the easily manipulated guy she had gotten the money from.

"You come over here all the time. Why? You're too young for...a lot of the reasons I can think of. But you don't really talk. You don't ask for anything. It doesn't make any sense."

I didn't understand her question. I had seen some people leaving her house and giving her money, so I assumed that they had some kind of specific purpose for their visits. However, I couldn't comprehend why she was confused about me. It was clear she only saw people for what they could give her. Those people provided her with money. She was capable of providing me with air-conditioning and cold drinks. "No. You're just nice."

She smiled. Maybe it's how I prefer to remember the moment, but I do think it was a genuine smile. She crossed the room and sat down next to me, so close to me that I could feel her leg pressing against mine. I began to slightly panic, because I wasn't accustomed to physical contact. My father had hugged me a couple of times, and my mother would rub my back against my will at night sometimes. I always assumed it was so they could tell themselves they were good parents. Still, to this day, I am not comfortable with physical, nonsexual intimacy.

Now, though, this older girl was intentionally sitting far too close for my own comfort. She looked at me and said, "You're really sweet. Here." She leaned even further into my personal bubble, and that was my first kiss.

I was extremely shocked and confused. I was already uncomfortable with physical contact, but this felt much more intimate and closer than anything I had experienced, and I didn't understand what she was attempting to do in that moment. I learned years later that this was apparently an atypical first encounter with the opposite sex. The first person I told was a girlfriend several years later, and she took the opportunity to inform me that what had occurred was technically an assault because of our age difference. She was appalled by the story. I understood her disgust with the girl, but I had already rationalized the incident. To a girl like her, physical affection was the only thing of value she had, and she wanted to be nice to me.

I hold no disdain for her, nor do I have any misgivings that she ever thought of me again after her family moved two years later. No further physical contact ever happened between the two of us. Even so, I still greatly appreciate her. She helped me realize that many people will use you if it can help them gain something. The only true method of protecting yourself is to use them first.

When I was ten, the first event that would eventually mold how I saw life, death, and myself occurred. It occurred right before my eyes. I was out walking the neighborhood, as I tended to do. There was a stray dog that I would see from time to time during these jaunts. He was old, with tattered gray hair and a tail that looked like it had been mangled in some fight or accident. I had discovered throughout my encounters with the dog that he seemed to be mostly blind and somewhat deaf. I'd named him Gray because I needed something to refer to him by, and because he had gray fur.

I was out walking one day when I saw Gray walking on the opposite side of the street. He limped along his path, ever mobile and never stopping. I had created the theory in my head that Gray had to always be walking because if he allowed himself to rest, he would die in that instant. His constant walking was a means of survival that he instinctively understood. I never once got in his way or tried to stop him to show him love. We were two kindred spirits, shunned from those who were socially obligated to protect us as youngins. Beaten and battered by our surroundings but still managing to devise our own methods of survival. I would like to think that Gray saw me in the same light—long-lost brothers of two different species, never interrupting the other's path but quietly acknowledging their existence.

On this day, I felt an odd urge. I wanted to call out to Gray. I don't know what came over me. Maybe he seemed particularly downtrodden, or maybe I was desiring company for my walk—a rarity at best. I stood across the paved road and called out to him, "Gray, come here, boy! Come here doggy and I'll give you a treat." Gray poked his head up in my general direction, guided more by the sound of my voice than his unreliable vision. I continued to call him, even going so far as to clap my hands and kneel to his level.

Gray seemed to feel more energized at this proposal for companionship. He turned his body and started to hobble across the road. His first few steps seemed livelier than I had ever seen him, and as he approached the middle of the road, I ceased my calls to see if he could still bridge the distance between us without the help of my voice. He started to slow down in the silence, continuing to stare at me the whole time.

It was then that the old steel-blue Honda Civic came down the road and smashed right into him.

Gray didn't yelp or howl. The grill of the vehicle made contact with his body for the briefest moment before he crumpled and was immediately introduced to the rubber tires on the driver's side of the car. The driver slammed on their brakes with a loud squeal as friction removed a fair amount of rubber from the bringers of Gray's end.

The woman rushed out of the car as I watched in curiosity. She was young, maybe college-aged, with long, blond hair. She had cut up the sides of her Nirvana T-shirt, and her jeans were full of holes, like she'd slashed them herself with a knife or scissors.

She ran to Gray's body, knelt down, and placed her hands on her head. I watched as this young woman experienced a range of emotions that I had not truly witnessed up to this point. I can identify them now that I am older, but at the time they seemed alien to me. She panicked, she froze, she grieved, and then she felt the rush of guilt set in. I watched as she cried for several minutes, causing her heavy mascara or eyeliner to create black lines down her face—black lines similar to the ones that traced from the front of her car back to Gray's corpse. Eventually, I became bored with the scene and continued my walk.

I never saw Gray again, of course. And I felt no sadness for him, nor guilt for calling to him, nor for stopping that call and stranding him there in the car's path.

Gray's life must have been miserable, and in a split second that misery disappeared. He didn't cry about his death, so why should I? That singular moment relieved him of all of his pain. If there was a victim in all of this, it was the driver. I still think about that young woman, and wonder if she remembers killing Gray or has dreams about that afternoon. The guilt that showed on her face would've been heartbreaking for anyone who could have understood her experience and felt empathy for her.

When my children's first dog died, I told them this story, and in a manner that conveyed more compassion and sadness than I felt on that day or any day since. But the story is not entirely true. There is a small lie in how I've told it over the years.

I had heard the car coming. I knew it would be driving down that same street that Gray and I were walking. I don't know if at that moment I wanted to see if Gray would sense the car's approach, or if he would be blind to it (literally and metaphorically speaking). I stopped calling his name when he arrived at the center of the road out of my own interest in what would happen. It didn't give me any sense of joy, and it most certainly did not provide some odd arousal or sexual awakening like serial killers in Hollywood movies.

I wish I could've read his mind at that moment. Maybe Gray's upturned head was a sign of appreciation for giving him the little encouragement he needed to end it all. Or maybe he was an old dumb dog that I lured to his death.

2

NOSTALGIA

I have never experienced nostalgia. There has never been a moment where I felt an emotion, other than anger, so strongly that I could experience that emotion again while remembering the inciting event. The emotional parts of my brain process situations different, and more often than not my emotional experience is blunted or completely numb. I don't grieve my inability to do this, because I don't think reliving situations is all that beneficial or important in life.

I don't have strong connections to my memories of childhood or the people that I was surrounded by. I don't think wistfully of my family's lack of connections. I don't experience grief or remorse about what happened to Gray. I don't even feel a longing for a different childhood that was not so poisoned by conflict and anger. I don't experience any resurgence of forlorn desires or unresolved emotion when I reflect on those times. Remembering and documenting my childhood is similar to describing your experiences grocery shopping. It is a summarization of the events and experiences without eliciting an emotional response.

I think that nostalgia holds back the vast majority of the people I have encountered. The strong grasp on the past keeps their focus on what existed before, and on constant attempts to recreate it for the future. Every decision I make is to move me to a new future that I wish to exist in. The past is gone; there is no use or reason to pine for it.

How many people sit around as adults wishing they could relive their glory days so they could be happy? And how many live lives pushed upon them by parental figures who are trying to relive their own nostalgia vicariously? I prefer the easier option; forget the past and figure out what makes me happy in the present. There's no point in pissing away half a life in order to experience what has already been experienced.

I also tend to have a skeptical view on nostalgic responses as a result of my profession as a psychiatrist. I have sat across from patients and heard their innermost secrets, the entirety of their life stories. At times, it seems I have listened to every story of family betrayal and abuse that could possibly exist.

It is exceedingly frustrating to listen to a young man describe his family as being wholesome and supportive, while simultaneously describing incidents where his father would get drunk nightly and launch insults at him like a rapid-fire machine gun. Perhaps even more difficult and puzzling is listening to a nice young woman blame herself for the dissolution of her marriage because he *had* to force her to have sex too often. The propensity for people to remember events or relationships through the tint of rose-colored glasses confounds me. Human memory confounds me. The strong emotions experienced during the few occasions of an abuser being nice can warp the memory of the relationship as a whole.

The only value something has is what it adds to the present. If I had $50 last year, it does nothing for me now. If I had an amazing first date three years ago, how does that date benefit me today? I had the experience, I learned what I could from it, and I have moved forward.

This perspective has benefited me more often than anyone who has better recall of their past. I have twisted and manipulated stories and statements with my wife in order to elude some unsavory consequences. I rarely remember the event strongly, so it is easier to invent a new story without having to navigate what I know is a lie. She will insist on a specific course of events, because she felt so strongly at that moment. I reinvent the moment from scratch because it wasn't important enough to remember, and that new story would be communicated with more confidence because it wasn't tainted by emotions.

I don't look back fondly; I move forward confidently. I don't wish for something that is lost; I seek what benefits me most now. If my memories are skewed or outright false, they're still true enough for me to accomplish my goals.

Adolescence—a truly horrible time in any person's existence. Sure, I was doing extremely well in school and was being approached yearly about participating in advanced programs. But I never took advantage of that other than taking a few high school classes during middle school. I didn't see a purpose in trying to achieve anything magnificent in my academics because my family was always telling me that I wouldn't amount to anything great.

Social situations were more difficult for me. I was starting to learn how to navigate the truly insane standards and rules of childhood friendships. The rules seemed fairly simple: find a common interest with the people around you, demean outsiders, and only be as visible as necessary to be considered part of the group. Certain social cliques were too difficult for me to infiltrate because I hadn't yet acquired the necessary understanding or patience to win over the members. The groups that seemed to dignify stupidity or place greater value on physical wealth were far too challenging for me at that age.

And all that was on the surface. Beneath the posturing and manipulation, I was completely inept. I didn't understand any reasons for the rules being set forth before me. Why did I need to have common interests with other people? Logically, it would make more sense to surround yourself with different people in hopes of being exposed to new hobbies or thoughts that better appeal to you. Why did I need to ostracize and belittle any outsiders? I disliked the outsiders the same amount as I disliked my peers within the group. The entire concept is a broken attempt at recreating tribal behaviors that existed in primitive man because the masses need to feel a sense of belonging. I feel nauseous even thinking about that concept.

So why did I subject myself to the process at all?

It was around this preteen era that I began to notice something was off kilter in my mind. I was watching as my peers clawed for attention and dominance. I noticed that people attempted to obtain this mantle of "leader of the pack" in a few different ways. Attractiveness to the opposite sex seemed to be a primary goal, so everyone around me was competing for this attention in manners that were frankly disgraceful. They also wanted to be viewed as the most desirable by the greatest number of people and would therefore act completely differently around different groups. It seemed a requirement to adorn a mask that was most appealing to the people in their immediate vicinity.

I found the entire social experiment to be odd and unproductive. I didn't want to be admired. I didn't want to maintain more relationships. I certainly had minimal interest in being viewed as some goal to aspire to by my peers. I didn't fully grasp how romantic relationships worked, and for a long time, those dynamics seemed to be more about what you could do for your partner and not what they did for you. I thought it was a complete waste of time dedicating energy to tempering the hormonal emotions of a girl just to have the trophy of girlfriend.

I knew I was struggling to make what others would define as appropriate friendships when I made my first friend—other than Gray. I was eleven when I met another boy who lived a few miles away. We'd originally met when I was breaking into a church during the summer.

It was a hot day, and I needed to use the restroom. There was a Baptist church on the block I was on, and considering it was the middle of the week, I assumed that it would be empty. I attempted to walk in, but the door was locked. I'm not sure if churches are supposed to keep people out of them, but I recognized it as a challenge. I had considered breaking into one of the houses on the street, but it was impossible to guarantee that it would be empty, and I had to pee bad enough that I didn't want to waste time running from a police officer.

I walked around the church to see if there were any other doors that could have been left open. What I found instead was another boy standing behind the church. I later found out that he was five years older than me and was standing there because that was where he would deal drugs during the weekdays.

He was wearing baggy clothes and had his brown hair spiked up. He saw me trying the doors and asked, "What are you doing back here kid? Shouldn't you be at home?"

Much like with the girl who gave me my first kiss, I was very confused by his question. I didn't understand why I would be at home, because I was always told kids should stay out of their house during the day.

"I'm just trying to get in here to pee."

I didn't think that the answer needed any further explanation, but he seemed confused, "Why don't you just piss on the outside then?"

"Because it's hot, there's A/C in there, and I thought maybe I could find some food also. All the doors are locked though."

The guy looked a bit amused. "Do you care how you get in?"

I shook my head. It didn't occur to me that there was a "wrong" way to get into the building. He walked to the parking lot and grabbed a rock, which he then threw like a baseball through a window next to the back door. "There. Let's go see if they got food."

We both climbed through the window. I found a restroom, and then we searched the building and found some of the snacks they must've set out before Sunday services. During our midday snack, we spoke and got to know one another.

He lived a few miles from my house and was in high school. He sold drugs on the days he skipped school because he wanted money to buy things like cigarettes from a gas station that didn't check his ID. I told him about myself, and he seemed interested in the fact that I spent the majority of my days by myself. After about an hour, we heard the creak of the heavy front door as it was pulled open. A middle-aged man saw us sitting in the pews and began yelling at us. We jumped up and ran for the window we'd entered through, then through the backyards of neighboring houses.

After that, we continued to hang out on almost a daily basis. I had made my first real friend, it seemed. The age difference didn't seem to bother either of us. He recognized that I wasn't judging him, and he was in no danger of me telling people about the things I would witness him doing, such as stealing and drugs.

Eventually, I realized that he was doing a lot and I was just an observer. I asked him what I could help with, and he took me under his wing. With two of us, it was easier to keep a look out for anyone who might catch him selling. He did everything he could to make money, and often complained about the struggles of being broke. I didn't really understand how much easier my life would be if I had more money, because money didn't change any of the struggles I wrestled with daily. Eventually, he grew tired of the small amounts of cash he would make with his various endeavors. One day, it escalated when he suggested that we go into a wealthier neighborhood, suggesting we might find some things to steal and sell. I didn't have any objections, because I was open to whatever activity if it meant staying out of the house.

While we were walking around, we saw two teenagers that were close to my friend's age. They were playing in their yard, and there was no car in the driveway. My friend walked over to them as I followed, and he confronted them. I barely paid attention at first, because the social aspect wasn't all that interesting to me. However, when voices started to get more aggressive, I became more focused, and I felt a surge of excitement rush through my body.

The whole thing resulted in my friend rushing one of the wealthier boys and hitting him hard in the jaw. I didn't need an invitation. I saw the other boy start to move, and I went on the attack. After we thoroughly decimated both boys, my friend told them to hand him all the money they had.

This became a new habit for us when the opportunity presented itself. Find teenagers that looked like they had money, corner them, beat them up, and take the money they had on them. Honestly, I was never really interested in the money and only ever spent it on food and cigarettes. I enjoyed the rush of holding a kid down and feeling my fist meet flesh while they lay there, helpless. I reveled in the accomplishment of the two of us being outnumbered by a group of four or five and still coming out on top. The black eyes, busted lips, and cracked ribs that I acquired throughout these experiences were never an issue for me. They were physical reminders of my own weakness, and motivation to get stronger and more capable.

As I entered middle school, we continued to be friends. When my peers would see him walking me to school, they would shoot concerned and confused looks in my direction. I didn't give their opinions any thought, because I enjoyed my time around him.

I guess it was something akin to loyalty. He never criticized or admonished me. He encouraged my interests. He offered me drugs once, but I wasn't interested and he never offered again. This was a respect of my boundaries that I hadn't experienced, and I found I greatly appreciated it.

He taught me that the world would never help me out and so I had to be okay getting what I wanted by any means. He taught me how to get away from the police with ease and to not let anyone infringe on my desires. He educated me in loyalty and honor among the disenfranchised. The rules for this community made much more sense to me. It was simple: do not tell on anyone, do not steal from or harm anyone you are close with, and do not trust anyone you haven't committed a crime with.

Two years after we met, he left town because he was finally an adult and his parents kicked him out of the house. I don't know what happened to him after that. I never saw a point in trying to find out. The relationship was based on and grew only based on what we could provide to one another. He was something like a role model to me. He taught me that it wasn't bad to accept who I was and what I wanted. I provided him with a lookout and backup when he was trying to earn money. Since he was gone, there was nothing more he could do for me.

•   •   •

With the loss of my only friend, and the onset of puberty, my major interest became girls. I still didn't see them as a method of expanding my popularity among peers, but my interest in sex rose rapidly. I realized that there was minimal chance of me experimenting with any of them if I was a complete social outcast, so I had to learn how to belong in order to get what I wanted. It was a process for me, but luckily, patience was my strong suit.

I observed the different groups and analyzed the behaviors of those that belonged. I was able to mimic the majority of it. I began mingling with different groups to see if any of them were more comfortable for me than the others. Sadly, I didn't find any of them to be more appealing than the others. I was able to mimic the different behaviors well enough, but none of it felt extremely natural for me. I felt like I had to be a completely different version of myself while hiding all of the traits I had developed with my friend during our time together.

I had my first girlfriend in the eighth grade. Teachers were still nagging me about joining classes for the academically advanced. I still didn't see much of a point, but I eventually agreed because I didn't see any potential downsides. I knew if I joined, it would get the adults to stop bothering me, which I saw as a net benefit. It was in one of the advanced math classes that I met her. She was my age, a gifted student and a cheerleader. She was much more popular than I was and had large groups of friends whom she was always around.

At some point during the year, she began trying to befriend me. She started off innocently enough: asking me for help with classwork, asking me about my weekend plans, etc. I was polite when she would ask. I provided short and concise answers, but I never interacted heavily. I wasn't sure why she was asking me all these questions or asking for my help. She must have been smart enough to be in the class, since she was allowed in. I didn't trust her random friendliness, so I kept a wall up while she spoke to me.

I didn't realize that she was flirting with me until another kid in the class pointed it out to me, but I was definitely interested. She was very pretty—below average height for a female, long brown hair that was always perfectly cared for, a thick build that I found more attractive than the extremely thin. She had a lot of friends, so dating her would introduce me to other girls I could pursue if the relationship failed.

I asked her out, and we dated for a few months. I was confused when I first learned that she was interested in me. Other than our academics, we had absolutely nothing in common. I rarely have a lot in common with the people around me, but she and I truly had nothing between us. She enjoyed being social, while I rarely socialized with anyone. She was a cheerleader and was involved in several school activities, and I tried to skip class as much as possible. She was also a devout Christian. I attempted to understand her reasoning as best as possible but continued to come up blank.

The relationship was bearable. She seemed nice

enough. She was attentive, and in the beginning, she wasn't judgmental or jealous. She did talk a lot and would occasionally ask for my clothing when she had to go out of town for whatever cheering event was going on. I thought that was odd at the time. I had always attempted to pick up the scent of people around me to see if there had been changes. I was able to tell a lot about a person based on changes in their scent: where they've been, who they've been with, what they've been doing. She only said she wanted something that smelled like me to remind her of me. It never really made sense.

I, on the other hand, was the ideal boyfriend in the beginning. I had watched other couples dating enough times that I understood the steps to keeping a partner interested and infatuated. I would write notes and fold them into inanely intricate designs and slip them into her locker. I would fill the notes with romantic song lyrics, compliments, the occasional statement of disbelief such as "I just don't understand what makes you so amazing," and of course childish drawings of hearts or winged babies equipped with bow and arrow. I didn't even understand what I was saying, but I knew it was the right thing to say because whenever I would do it, I would get to grope and make out with her.

We never went so far as to have sex, no matter how much I tried. She was a decent kisser and always wanted to dry hump. She never admitted it, but I always assumed it was some type of religious obligation to stay "pure" until marriage. I never grasped why penetration was the moment that purity was extinguished.

Apparently, God had no issue with her being shirtless and trying her damnedest to reach climax through two layers of denim, but actually succeeding by removing the barriers of cloth would be a hellworthy trespass. And I was the ridiculous one?

The end of the relationship was inevitable for a number of reasons, the first of which was my level of patience listening to friendship drama. I found it to be a complete waste of my mental energies and eventually had a difficult time not showing that irritation. I didn't have anything to add to those conversations. I had a few social relationships, but nothing so significant that I would care if I heard they were gossiping about me. Betrayal can only occur if there is a certain level of attachment or trust, and I had not committed enough crimes with any of them to build trust.

Second was simply the nature of time, and how it reveals all things. I never truly changed. I continued to smoke, still got into fights, refused to go to church with her, and had absolutely no interest in getting to know her friends better.

In one argument, I had walked to her house to spend time with her, and we were sitting on her bed side-by-side. She was complaining about some friend or another being rude to her in the hall at school. I honestly don't remember what it was about because I wasn't paying attention. She apparently noticed and got angry with me. "Are you even listening to me?"

I noticed the change in tone. I wanted to lie, but on that day, I could no longer put my "good boyfriend" mask on. "Honestly, no. I got confused while you were telling me the story and I didn't want to ask you to explain it to me."

Her face became red with anger, and the metaphorical steam began pouring out of her ears. "What is wrong with you? I'm trying to tell you what's going on with me, and you can't even support me."

I paused, sensing that this was the breaking moment. "How do I support you when someone else is talking about you, but you refuse to say anything to them? There's always something going on with you, and honestly, it's all completely stupid. You're like an annoying child when you do this." My response was calm and apathetic. I knew the moment I gave her a glimpse behind my mask that the relationship would end.

Indeed, her face froze in shock and tears started to swell in her eyes. Her mouth hung slightly agape. I had seen pain on several people's faces in the midst of fights, but this was different. She wasn't in pain; she was emotionally hurt.

I didn't immediately recognize the effect it had on me. Later I would recognize it as the first time I felt it. Behind the surface of my thoughts, my blood began to pump faster, and an urge to keep pushing rose from somewhere I had never explored. I felt powerful knowing that I could crush her entire concept of reality with mere words. I was aroused.

She gathered herself, and the hurt was replaced with anger. "I'm the child?" Her voice rose until it became a shriek. "You run around like the rules don't apply to you. What is wrong with you? I thought you were a really interesting guy. You were smart and you didn't care about all the stupid stuff other boys do. But apparently, you don't care about anything at all. You're just broken."

I allowed her to finish her temper tantrum. I stared into her eyes with a cold, lifeless stare. Her words and her tone didn't intimidate me. It was like being growled at by a chihuahua. She was no threat to me, but something about her words struck the flint in those depths. A heat spread from my gut to my extremities, and I felt an emotion I had never experienced—pure rage. A desire to destroy the person in front of me.

I stood up slowly and positioned myself in front of her. She was trapped on that bed as I towered over her. My gaze was cold, showing no hint of the burning furnace. "I'm broken? You think you know anything about me?" I questioned her in a low and calm tone. I wanted to show her that if she was the chihuahua, I was the rottweiler; my fangs had already tasted flesh.

Her face changed again. Her eyes were wide, and it was like her breathing stopped. I imagined grabbing her by the throat and repeatedly slamming my fist into her face until that looked disappeared. "Don't fool yourself. You're just someone I used to get what I wanted. You've been nothing but an object to me this whole time."

Time stopped moving. She was frozen in front of me. My words had struck something in her and destroyed it. Eventually, I picked up my hoodie and left.

It was a six-mile walk, which gave me plenty of time to process what I had just experienced. The intense sensations had faded the moment I walked away. I knew that the things she was saying should have hurt me, but I hadn't felt hurt—I had wanted to hurt her. Not like the way my mother would hurt us to make herself feel superior or the way I hurt the kids when taking their money. I wanted to do it simply because I was angry and it would make me happier. And I didn't hate the feeling.

As far as I knew, she never told anyone about that day. She might have told people we broke up or that I was an asshole, but I don't think she told anyone about exactly what she saw in me.

She would avoid me at school, though, and her friends would shoot hateful looks in my direction when passing me. It ruined my chances at interacting sexually with any of her friends. I had a few more girlfriends during the remaining months of middle school and the first year of high school, but they were all short lived. The girls were either too boring, too intellectually simple, or too dramatic for me to waste my time on.

I refocused my social experimentation efforts to drugs and alcohol. By the time I entered high school, I had already had plenty to drink, but had never actually been drunk and hadn't experimented with drugs. Both of my sisters had heavily used different drugs—specifically LSD, ecstasy, and crystal meth. Probably many others that I was unaware of. I had seen them recovering the morning after a night of overindulgence to the point they couldn't move. I agreed to try marijuana on a few occasions, but not a significant amount. The feeling was nice, but I didn't understand the scale of the positive reviews. I didn't understand the concept of basing an entire culture around the use of the drug that caused one to be lethargic and hungry. Being drunk was slightly different, because there were stages of intoxication that could either help me have an easier time socializing or, conversely, make my violent urges more difficult to manage. It was a fun challenge to balance the effects and learn my own limitations.

When I entered high school, I was able to find a place with a group of others who regularly used drugs and alcohol in excess. They weren't the most popular, which was fine by me. I pretended to like the same things as them, like *World of Warcraft* or punk music, when in reality I didn't care for any of that. I mostly chose this group because they were easy to manipulate.

They were all older than me by a year or two, so they all saw themselves as mentors to me. I didn't mind the occasional condescension if it meant they would buy me lunch or use their relationships with teachers to get me out of classes. The only person in the group I truly detested was the de facto "leader." He was arrogant and wanted to receive attention and adulation from everyone around him. When he did something for another person, he expected to be praised. He kept his hair short but would obviously spend tireless time molding it to look as if he had just gotten out of bed without styling. His build was physically smaller than mine—shorter by a couple of inches and at least twenty pounds lighter—but he still acted as if he were physically superior.

The most annoying part of this boy was the way he marched his girlfriend around with him. They had been dating for several years when I met him, and he acted like that gave him some badge of proficiency that gave him the right to give advice on love to everyone who would listen. He would tell me all the time which girls I should ask out and how to keep a girlfriend, as if he knew me enough to know what attracted me.

His girlfriend herself was alright. She was fairly quiet (my guess is she had to be, since he never stopped talking). She had very long black hair and was extremely thin. Often, she wore baggy black pants with holes in them and safety pins climbing the side like a ladder to her thighs. She usually had on one of her boyfriend's shirts, but I wasn't sure if that was by choice or his request. Overall, I found her mildly attractive, but not really my type.

That didn't stop me from losing my virginity to her.

I grew very tired of the boy's behavior and so I thought a fitting punishment for acting superior to me was to bring him down to my level. I never wanted to show that I was the better man, I just wanted him to see the world how I saw it. So, I began speaking to his girlfriend in classes that he wasn't in. I put on the nice and innocent guy act, because I had a suspicion that it would help this meek and mild target feel more at ease. I took an interest in everything she talked about and played ignorant, while encouraging her to tell me about what she enjoyed. This allowed her to feel more empowered and confident, like she'd found her voice and was on equal footing with someone. It was only a couple weeks of this routine before I saw the signs of attraction in her eyes.

So, I started to address the differences I saw between her behavior in our solo conversations and when we were in a group. This led to her complaining about how her boyfriend would steamroll every conversation. I would offer the basic platitudes of "that must be so hard" and "you really do deserve better," which she devoured like a starving puppy. I began to address her more directly in group settings where her boyfriend was present, like at lunch. She would typically sit there quietly, but I would ask her opinions on the conversations to further ingratiate her to me.

The process took a lot of effort. I knew she was so entangled with him that she wouldn't betray him without sufficient reason. Whereas with my first kiss and my first girlfriend, everything was handed to me on a platter, this girl made me work for what I wanted—and I did rather enjoy the hunt.

At some point, she started becoming angrier at her boyfriend, and they were soon arguing on an almost daily basis. Each night, I would stay up with her on the phone and comfort her. I knew what I was doing the entire time, but it never occurred to me that it was wrong or hurtful. I would reflect on my actions in the safety of my journals, but never once arrived at the conclusion that this was a taboo that I should have steered away from. I wanted him to hurt, I wanted to have sex, and I wanted his girlfriend to willingly betray him for me. In that sense, it was simple.

It was three days after my fourteenth birthday when

I accomplished my goal. She called me to offer a belated happy birthday and asked about how I celebrated on the actual day and what my plans were that night. I told her that I didn't really celebrate my birthdays, which was true. Most years, I would spend my birthday alone watching horror movies. I understood the concept that a birthday was supposed to be special (even if I didn't fully grasp why it should be), and my parents were usually at work or attending to their own interests. I took the opportunity to get away from the stress of interacting and watch graphic violence by myself. It was what I preferred. Why should surviving another rotation around the sun be celebrated with a party?

She asked me if I could come over since she was feeling upset and lonely due to the most recent altercation with her boyfriend. She told me that her parents were gone for the weekend, and she didn't want to be alone.

I agreed and rode my bike to her house, curious how far this would go. As soon as I arrived, she pounced on me like a lioness on her kill. I didn't stop her or try to slow her down. We went at it for an hour before I got dressed and left.

This went on for several weeks, always meeting in private at her house or mine. By this time, my parents were rarely home, so it was easy to go there night or day. And it was fun, obviously. I was a teenage boy having sex as much as I wanted with a girl who only wanted my attention half the time because the other half she was with her boyfriend. I didn't see the downside.

After the first time, I didn't feel any closer to her, which was weird because up to this point, everything I'd seen and heard talked about the spiritual and emotional component of sex. I thought maybe it was because it was my first time, but it never developed after any of the subsequent encounters either. I saw having sex with her as a purely physical means of obtaining pleasure. It was more effective and enjoyable than any solo method.

In contrast, I could see the growing emotional attachment she was experiencing. She was wanting to cuddle more after each session, which I found to be very uncomfortable. I didn't enjoy physical touch unless there was a purpose behind it, and there is no real purpose in cuddling. It was worth it for the time being because I was still getting what I wanted, but all good things must come to an end.

One day, she came to my house after school, and the purpose was clear. We were in the middle of the act when I heard a knocking at my door. My first thought was that it was my sister coming to bitch at me about making too much noise, and I prepared myself to tell her to go to hell. My partner quickly grabbed her small Superman panties and slipped them on, but I wasn't too concerned about her privacy as I opened my bedroom door. I stood there in boxers while she was still trying to get her second leg through the hole of the underwear, and staring straight at me was her boyfriend. My sister must've let him into the house, the bitch.

His look was pure anger, and I'm sure if he wanted, it would've killed me then and there. I stood there staring at him. I tried to process how I should respond and found myself surprised I hadn't considered this possibility. I could've gotten angry about him having the gall to stand in my house with that attempt at intimidation on his face. I could've been protective of her and defended that she was not to be blamed. I could've tried to play guilty and innocent while denying any intention or forethought.

I decided to proceed with, "Yeah? What do you need?"

The boyfriend began yelling, "What the hell are you doing?" He looked past me to his girlfriend. "Get your clothes on. We're leaving!"

I considered defending her and saying she could stay if she wanted, but I was too curious about how this was going to play out. I stayed silent and looked back at her as she continued putting her clothes back on. The very hurry with which she acted seemed to inhibit her urgency. I looked back at him, and he was staring into my eyes. His face was completely red, and tears were in his eyes. "I should kick your ass right now," he pushed through clenched teeth. That brought a smile to my face.

"You can try," I responded. I could see his fists clenching, but he was holding himself back. Still curious how this might end, I wanted to push the envelope. "I just don't get how it took you so long to figure this out."

His fist rose, and that was all the invitation I needed. I grabbed the side of his head and pushed while stepping into the hallway. I pushed forward with all my strength and shoved his head through the drywall opposite my bedroom. A hole about three inches in diameter formed as his skull made contact with a loud *thud*. I held his head there with my right hand as I brought my left up into face. I felt that same urge to hurt him. His girlfriend's presence behind me disappeared from my mind. I thought of every time he'd spoken to me like he could run my life better than me and every time he'd pretended like his life was so perfect. I knew he was emotionally scarred by the scene of his girlfriend mostly naked in another man's room, but I wanted him to have a physical scar to remind him every single day for the remainder of his life.

"Stop it, now!" The voice of the younger of my sisters rang through the hall. I paused and looked to my left, where she had been standing to watch and enjoy the show. That single momentary hesitation was enough to allow my logic to return. I looked behind me, and his girlfriend was standing there in my room, terrified. Her hands hung at her side, trembling. I looked down at the boyfriend, his eyes open but betraying the daze of his head injury. His anger had dissipated, and his expression was almost blank. My left hand hurt as the adrenaline emptied from my system.

"Both of you, get the fuck out of my house. If you threaten me again, I'll kill you," I said with a heavy weight of repressed anger hanging on the words. Both of them skulked out of the house without saying another word.

My sister stood in the hallway for another moment before leaving silently. I stayed frozen in place, trying to bring my body and emotions under control. The entire incident ran through my mind. I slept with another person's girlfriend, he found out, and I wanted to kill him. Then I hung my head as I muttered, "Dad is going to kill me for putting a hole in the wall."

LOVE

ove. True love. In love. Love of your life. Love between friends. Parental love. There are a nauseating amount of ways the word gets used. It is often the pivotal focus of music and cinema. Yet despite it being such a commonplace term, used daily by almost any verbal human, I don't think the vast majority of people can even define it.

For a very long time, I didn't believe love existed. It was just a hopeful notion that kept people paying for expensive dates or helping friends move. We are told that parents have an almost genetic obligation to love their offspring, but I'm not the only one who saw the vacant and loveless eyes of their parents. Romantic love is supposed to be special and eternal, yet people still have multiple affairs or build resentment for their partner.

There have been several individuals who entered

and departed my life, but those departures never affected me. When I left home, I was not affected in the slightest by the absence of my parents or siblings. Friends, girlfriends, peers, and coworkers all exited from my life, and I never stumbled.

I find it repugnant that the word is used so casually. If love is as beautiful and special as people say, it should only be used in the most limited fashion. It can't be used for every single friend that you have. If every person you connect with has your love, then love itself is not special. Needing someone in your life is not love, it's reliance. You depend on the scaffolding of your relationships to function.

I don't understand what is so unacceptable about being honest with other people that we only care about them because of what they offer us. A friend with money offers fun. A friend with status offers acceptance. People look for how they benefit in relationships before they even begin them. People have to lie about these factors. No one wants to feel like the people who care for them only do so because they are the most convenient option.

Love is the ambiguous bandage that we use to hide the ugly scars of what caused us to form the relationship. We can fall back on that word to explain away any doubts of our motivations to do things for people, without ever actually explaining it. When the socially awkward girl asks her popular friend why she's being invited to go out, it's harmful if the popular girl answers, "Because standing next to you increases my chances of looking pretty and finding a cute boy." So, instead, we rely on the statement, "Because I love you."

A parent's love for their child has two extra factors. Parents love their children because of biology and because they are told they should love their children. What is inherently lovable about a seven-pound ball of wrinkled flesh that does nothing but cry, poop, and sleep? They're basically puppies that don't alert you when someone is at the door. I didn't feel immediate waves of affection for my children the moment they were expelled from the womb. However, innumerable parents will look at their child two days after it's born and exclaim how much they love it. What do you love? Or is it possible that years of conditioning that babies should be loved, solely because they are babies, creates an involuntary obligation to care for something that offers no benefits.

I love my wife because she's the only female my age I can bear to listen to without getting a headache. If socializing is a necessity in life, then I want to do it with someone that matches my intellect. I love my children because they are substantially better to interact with than most people. They have zero expectations of what I should be as a person, and they provide me a chance to feel like I'm not solely a monster. These are the benefits of the relationships and what makes the relationship attractive to me.

In relationships, once a person has declared they love the other person, the love becomes the justification to endure shit treatment. People will stay in unhealthy relationships solely because they think they love someone. Even when the attraction disappears and the benefits of the relationship have run dry, the sensation of love can remain if the person has convinced themselves. In their minds, love is too significant to be a response that can just vanish due to changing circumstances. So, they hold on to love as a reason to be subjected to dehumanizing treatment.

The majority of murders, after all, are committed by close friends or family.

The remainder of my high school social life essentially ended after the fight. The boyfriend told everyone that I was a psycho, and the stories about me grew out of control. The original story was fairly close to the truth, but then I started hearing more and more outlandish versions. There was one where the girlfriend tried to stop me from beating him and I ended up attacking her. There was one where he caught me assaulting her and tried to be the hero. There was one in which I pulled a knife and started cutting myself to intimidate them.

I had no interest in sexually assaulting anyone; rape is crass, the action of a man who feels less than and has something to prove. The one about me cutting myself was offensive because I really didn't understand it. Why would I cut myself to intimidate someone else? I would have stabbed him—that is clearly more threatening. I never understood what was scary about a person standing there bleeding in front of others. The mind of teenagers is an unorganized cluster of illogical ideas and rumors.

Regardless, after the rumors spread, no one had any interest in being my friend. I was shunned in the hallways, and fellow students would shout obscenities at me. I didn't mind so much, but I was a tad disappointed. I had put forth a great amount of effort to cultivate shallow relationships, and they were all uprooted solely because I acted impulsively and was caught.

I knew I had no right to blame anyone else for the results of my actions; I had broken the rules. I wanted to point the finger at others and explain how they were just as at fault as me, but more for my edification than to earn a spot of belonging again. I decided that if high school was basically over for me, I would dedicate myself to doing well academically and leaving school early.

I was still human, however, so I was still interested in sex. I no longer trusted myself to try to form a relationship that involved recurrent exposure to each other. I was honestly somewhat scared of what had happened to me. I knew I had hurt people before, and had enjoyed it, but in all those situations I had gained something, such as money. That was the first time I was excited to physically hurt someone just for the sake of seeing them in pain. Later I realized that I had forgotten how much pleasure I received from watching that first girlfriend be hurt. I concluded that I separated them in my mind because hers was just an emotional pain, so she should've been able to recover quickly. I decided I should avoid any close social entanglements to help avoid whatever had triggered that response.

I would find a girl I thought was attractive and use my natural gift of manipulation to lure them into bed. I never intended for any encounter to happen a second time. Once the hunt was completed, and the trophy was gained, I didn't see a point in returning.

I didn't give a great deal of consideration to how that would affect the girls. I once seduced a girl that was a couple of years older than me and then was too tired afterward to drive her home, so I told her to walk. I didn't see anything particularly wrong with that, because she came over with an understanding of the intent, and that's what she got.

I did find an interesting phenomenon with females in my age range. Manipulation was surprisingly easy. I found that when I removed my mask somewhat and simply looked at a girl the way I actually saw her, she would start to melt. I always thought I had to hide myself, to pretend that when I looked at them I saw someone I respected and appreciated. I had to pretend to care about their friendship drama, their hopes, their fears. However, with some I would look at them like the conquest they represented to me. I would give them the predatory glance that a tiger uses while stalking prey, and they were happy to do whatever I asked.

Home life hadn't changed much. Everyone still hated each other, and no one spoke without some form of hostility or manipulation. My oldest sister had moved away the moment she was able, and I had limited contact with her as she was building her own life away from the toxicity of our bloodline. My younger sister became heavily addicted to drugs and eventually attempted suicide a few times. It didn't have any great influence on me. I would wake up to a scene of one of her attempts and the house being empty, clean up whatever mess of pill bottles or blood was there to avoid getting yelled at for not doing chores, and then go about my day.

This dynamic actually made my life considerably better. My parents were arguing more with the absence of my oldest sister and the changes in the balance of the household. When they weren't arguing about that, they were solely focused on my other sister and either getting her clean or keeping her alive. My parents would check in on me on occasion, but it was obvious that it was normally out of obligation instead of genuine interest. I was allowed to live without the confines of their oversight.

I used this newfound freedom to get myself my first job. I was somewhat...inspired by my oldest sister's ability to work for her own financial independence. Plus, I had no interest in throwing parties or sitting around high all day long. Making money seemed like the most logical decision.

I took a job as a waiter at a restaurant, because it was available and seemed like easy work. I had to put on the same mask that I was accustomed to wearing the majority of the time and smile at annoying strangers in order to get what I wanted—the perfect job for me. This restaurant was willing to hire sixteen-year-olds as wait-staff because they didn't serve alcohol. However, I wasn't like the other teenagers they hired; I didn't care about standing in the kitchen gossiping about mind-numbing banalities. I was showing up to work, and therefore I worked.

I was quickly given extra responsibilities, such as setting up the buffet every Sunday morning for the religious crowd. The person in charge had to be at work several hours before everyone else in order to prep, and without a lot of supervision. My supervisor trusted me solely based on the misunderstanding that my lack of social interest was actually a strong work ethic. I made sure to do well with the buffets, though. I wanted to maintain the job since it allowed me to work for hours without the obligation of interacting with other people.

I think that my supervisor at that job might have been the first person I genuinely respected. He would regularly ask me to change shifts or handle tasks that other people were struggling with. One day, he asked me if I could possibly do a day shift because several people had quit. I agreed; after all, at this point school was mostly pointless. I was making almost perfect grades without paying attention, and my teachers were becoming frustrated at how easily the material came to me.

The day shift was primarily adults, and the pacing of the work was completely different. How they communicated throughout the shift and how they supported each other functioned at an entirely different level. After the shift, my supervisor called me into his office and sat me down. I wasn't worried. I knew that I'd done well throughout the shift, and I merely assumed that he wanted to ask for some other schedule adjustment. My supervisor was an extremely tall Black man, easily four or five inches taller than me. He kept his head shaved smooth and his suit pressed. He always seemed to be professional, yet he was ready to make jokes and efficiently calm difficult situations without hesitation.

As I entered, he asked me to sit down, then leaned back in his seat and asked, "What are you, exactly?"

The question caught me off guard. It made no sense. I had gotten strange questions at school, but no one here had been apprised of my past behaviors. So I looked back, matching his calm. "I thought I was a waiter. Am I wrong?"

He chuckled slightly. "No, you aren't wrong. But I haven't seen someone do what you did today. You're some kind of chameleon."

Still assessing the vagueness behind what I interpreted to be an accusation, I proceeded hesitantly. "I don't know what you mean, boss. I just worked my shift. If I did something wrong, tell me."

His face contorted into confusion. "No, nothing was wrong. That's what was weird. I wanted you to work this shift so that you could be pushed to keep up. These guys work faster and harder than the teenagers at night. So, I thought you'd enjoy seeing a different work pace and maybe pick up a thing or two. But you"—he snapped his fingers—"picked it up like it was nothing. You just adapted to it and kept up. I didn't see that coming. Wanted to tell you good job."

I had never had someone watch me like that and notice my behaviors. I took pride in being able to adapt to my environment because it made manipulating those around me easier, but no one had ever noticed before. And he didn't just notice that I was wearing my mask; he caught a glimpse of what was under it and was impressed by it.

I was impressed by his perceptiveness. I was also intimidated. I didn't like the feeling of being seen and figured out. I had never felt intimidated before. So out in the open, so vulnerable. I was accustomed to direct conflict, yelling, physical attacks. I was not comfortable knowing that this person was watching and learning about me. I didn't know why, but I felt like his knowledge of how I adapt was some sort of threat to me. My mask was my secret, and if he wanted, he could tell people about it.

I continued to work my shifts there, alternating between day and night. I even managed to make a friend. He was more of an acquaintance, because we never interacted outside of work, but he was simple enough that there were minimal expectations in our interactions. He was a Bosnian kid who was seventeen years old. He was physically much larger than me, but there was never any moment of contest between us. I think we had a mutual level of respect for each other; me for his life experiences in Bosnia during a war and him for the fact that I wasn't intimidated by him. He was no stranger to people keeping a distance from his large build and imposing attitude. He wasn't watching me like our boss, though. He never played a major role in my life until the day I lost my first job.

It was a Sunday, and I had gotten to the restaurant at 6 a.m. to begin doing all of the buffet prep work. Everything went as normal. During the lunch shift, it was my responsibility to keep the buffet fully stocked and keep preparing items that were running low. This required a lot of moving around and going back and forth from the kitchen. I remember this one day specifically because of how it ended. For some reason, there was one major stressor that was pushing me physically to my limits: strawberries. Everyone was eating the strawberries, and I had to cut them a certain way before putting them out. It was annoying, sure, but not enough to put me into a place of anger.

There was a hostess my age that had been working there a year longer than me. She and I had never had any issues with each other, other than she had asked me on a date and I said no because I didn't want another situation like my last two "relationships" to occur at work. This specific Sunday, though, she was testing my patience. She was insistent on telling me what I needed to do and what I was doing wrong throughout the entire shift.

I had snapped before. My first girlfriend had spent weeks pushing my nerves, then made a verbal attack custom tailored to push off-limits buttons. The boyfriend of the later girl had crossed a serious line by coming into my house and threatening me. These snaps had occurred only in response to an extreme trigger. What happened next was different. I don't know if it was something about her, or the consequences of me not noticing my increasing stress.

I remember the next experience as clearly as if it happened yesterday. I was standing in the dining area, pouring more of those damn strawberries into the serving container. The Bosnian was there helping out with some of the other refills because of how busy we were. The rejected female coworker came into the dining area and stood about fifteen feet away from me with her hands placed on her hips and her face betraying every bit of attitude she was about to give me.

"What are you doing? Are you stupid? You need to help more with the tables," she shouted at me from that distance. There was a lot of noise in the restaurant, so only the most immediate tables could hear her words. I didn't feel embarrassed or condescended to; I felt the same rage that was now becoming more familiar.

I hung my head for a moment, trying to collect myself. I felt rage building within me, and I wanted to lash out. I took a deep breath and turned to face her. When I responded, my voice was noticeably louder and more aggressive than hers, "Shut your mouth, bitch, or else."

Her face was only shocked for a slight moment before displaying her own anger. She stayed planted in spot. "What are you going to do about it? Nothing."

Who did she think she was? She thought she had the right to challenge me. She thought that she could call me out in the middle of this dining hall and I would tuck my tail between my legs and walk away with a mumbled "whatever." But I did not.

I grabbed the metal quarter pan that was sitting next to me and threw it straight at her. It flew past her head without striking her, sadly. My voice wasn't loud, but it was aggressive. The bass of my voice allowed it to carry across the now silent dining area, whose noise was shattered by the clang of the pan. "I'm going to beat you to death with my bare hands!" I moved forward. My steps were reflexive to the anger I was feeling. She had no right to speak to me that way, and I was going to show her the consequences. My hands morphed into fists, and I was ready to follow through on my threat to its full extent.

Suddenly, two massive arms wrapped around me and lifted me off the ground. I heard the Bosnian speak loudly but calmly, "Don't do it." He placed me back down but kept me in a bear hug. I stood there seething, staring at the frightened look of the person I wanted to hurt. I was angry, not because of what I was doing but because someone was stopping me.

"You don't want to get arrested here," he added. "Come outside and I'll give you a cigarette."

The cigarette was tempting, but his logic that doing this in front of witnesses would surely land me in handcuffs actually pierced the armor of my anger. My mind raced, measuring the benefits and consequences of my actions. I released the tension in my muscles, and the Bosnian released me. He stayed with me and escorted me out back, where he pulled out two cigarettes and handed me one.

I was obviously fired. As much as my supervisor appreciated my work, apparently threatening to kill an employee where customers could hear was a no-exception rule.

I had to make a decision that day while I was on my way home. I had long known the differences between me and other people. I now had to accept the fact that my desire to hurt others was growing. It was becoming more difficult to control and was being set off by less intense situations. I made the decision to ask my parents for help, like maybe going to see a counselor. It was uncomfortable asking them and having to admit out loud the parts of me I had tried so hard to hide. I knew I would be lumped into the same category of "disturbed" as my sister, but at this rate, I would really end up killing someone and spend my life in prison.

I pulled up to the house and parked my car. I steeled myself for the conversation, then walked into the house.

It was empty. There was no note or any indication of when anyone would return. I went to my room and grabbed the bottle of vodka I kept under my bed and my pack of Newports. Only one thought flashed through my head as the warm liquor mixed with the taste of tobacco in my mouth. *That was a stupid idea. I don't need help.*

I never mentioned what happened with the job to my family, and they never noticed that I had lost it. I never asked for help, and in the time after being fired, I settled back into accepting myself for who I was. I didn't feel defeated by the fact there was no one around to support me. In fact, I'd had an epiphany when I walked into that empty house. There was no one who could help me. I had spoken to enough people and heard their opinions on how those who are different should be treated—ostracized or forced to fit the mold. The people around me would have been inept or impotent in any attempts to help me, because I wouldn't have entertained suggestions about being the same as everyone else.

I sat in my bed, drinking and smoking, and realized that everyone I've ever met was easily manipulated or obsessed with external validation. After consideration, I didn't think therapy would have any effect. The therapists I had seen on television or movies were all far too compassionate and sympathetic for me to be comfortable with. If therapists were that caring, it also meant they were that much easier to manipulate. Worse yet, if I decided to be completely forward and honest with a therapist and they started to judge me, that could easily be the final interaction where I truly lost control.

I began spending less time around people as a means of controlling any aggressive urges or desires that I might have had. School was particularly difficult, because even if I stayed to myself, I was still surrounded by potential targets with unpredictable behaviors. Those behaviors could stoke the fire that I was trying to dowse. I approached my vice principal and asked him what I could do to graduate as early as possible. I needed to move on from this point of my life; I didn't fit in with that environment.

It took some convincing, but he told me that he could provide the answers if I could return and tell him what my plan was after high school. His requirements were irritating but understandable. I had been to his office on several occasions for the different rumors he had heard, but he had noticed that I was grounded, calm, and not escalating situations on school grounds. So, me making such an odd request could've been seen as me trying to escape the stressors of my peers without any logical thought.

Truthfully, I had never given that much thought to my future. I had only ever thought of escaping my current situation, working some, and finding a life where I could avoid the horrors of everyday social interactions. However, in order to live a life of complete self-reliance, I needed to first be financially independent.

I smoked a decent amount of weed that night and reflected on what careers would be plausible for me. I didn't want to just do it to appease the vice principal; I thought it was helpful information for me as well. I continued to isolate further out of fear of what would happen, but that would only result in me eventually being unable to work and being dependent on others. This was unacceptable, and it contradicted everything I had learned in my life up to this point.

I knew I wanted to have a sense of authority so that no one would attempt to challenge me and potentially set off that darker side. Any job where I would be expected to carry a weapon would most definitely result in incarceration. I wanted to primarily work alone so that I wouldn't have colleagues who might allow their own bad day to affect me. I thought of the careers that I had been exposed to and what I thought of each of them. My father was a paramedic, but that was unlikely to be a good fit. I didn't know if I would care enough to try hard to save someone's life. My mother worked in a doctor's office, but she constantly complained about interacting with scores of people each day. Then, I remembered the night I was fired, and I felt confident with my answer.

The next day, I walked into my vice principal's office, looked him in the eyes, and said, "I'm going to be a psychiatrist." My answer was confident and unwavering. I stared down at him as he sat at his desk.

He leaned back slightly. "Interesting answer. Why?"

I think he wanted to challenge me, to see if I was giving an answer that was designed to make him happy or one that I actually desired. "I don't like interacting with too many people at a time; this will be primarily one-on-one. It is a field of science, and my science grades have never been questioned. And I think the majority of people in that field are completely incompetent, and I plan to be different." My gaze never left his. My answer wasn't purely deceptive. What I said was partially true. I omitted the fact that I hated that I would still have to interact with people, but interactions with patients would be easier to digest because they would be focused on accomplishing a goal and not on socializing.

We stared at each other for a minute before he reached into his desk. He handed me packets of paperwork and explained that there was a program where I could take tests to receive high school credits for each test passed. He explained that the tests would cover the entire year's worth of instruction and would be very difficult. He told me that if I wanted to graduate at the end of the year, I would need to pass six tests within a month, and each test cost $50.

I told him I would have the money by the end of the week. Then I returned to class and finished out my day, only paying slight attention to the teacher. The priority for my attention was making $250 by the end of the week. I could rob a few people, sell some of my parents' and sister's belongings, or sell whatever drugs and alcohol I had in my room. It might be tight because of the timeframe, but I would make it happen.

I had no concerns over the difficulty of the exams, because I had never failed an exam. I had read several of my textbooks from cover to cover out of boredom and curiosity, and the majority of schoolwork was easy. Even in those later years, they build off of the foundation that is taught at lower levels in a logical sense. As long as I had a strong foundation, which I did, I could use deductive reasoning to find solutions to problems I hadn't been exposed to.

When I left school that day, I opted to not go home. I wanted to drive around and stay to myself for a bit. I had a plan for my future. It filled me with what I assumed was excitement. I hadn't been excited about my future before, but the longer I thought about graduating, going to college, and then becoming a psychiatrist, the more I looked forward to it. I wanted to stay away from my house; I couldn't let my family ruin my mood.

It wouldn't be the first time I'd heard that I wouldn't amount to anything.

I drove my dark green Ford Taurus all over the city until nightfall. I knew I still had to pay for the tests, pass them, and graduate, but for the first time I felt like this place wasn't going to be the dungeon that my chains kept me stuck in. I passed by the church that I had broken into, drove down the street that Gray died on, my first girlfriend's house, and even my first job. Eventually the sun set, and the city became dark. I decided that it would be safe to return home and get some sleep. I would worry about taking action on the money later.

I pulled up to a stop sign a couple of miles from my house. The streetlights often didn't work on my street, so it was difficult to see. I turned left at the intersection, and as my car straightened itself into the lane of the small road, I heard a loud bang and felt my car jump. It took my brain a full second to process what had happened before I hit my brake pedal. Images of Gray lying on the road lifeless passed through my mind. My heart began to race as I tried to process what was happening. I decided it was best to get out of the car and clear up any uncertainties.

I slowly got out and walked to the front. The bumper on the passenger's side had a large dent in it. Then I continued around that side.

Even though it was dark, I could immediately identify what I was looking at. It was the body of an adult male. He was wearing a black jacket and hat, as well as darker jeans. I hadn't seen him crossing the street when I made the turn.

I approached his body to get a closer look and check for his vitals. I turned his face to look at me and his eyes hung open, staring directly at me. His face was dirty, and his beard was patchy and ill-kept. It seemed, based on his vacant, nonblinking stare, that he was no longer alive.

The same images of Gray appeared in my mind, accompanied by the same curiosities. Did this guy cross the street at night dressed in dark clothing hoping to get hit? Maybe he was homeless and didn't want to live anymore. Maybe he was depressed and tired of dealing with his life. I started to search his body to see if there was any identification that could provide more clues. I found his wallet in one of his back pockets. I opened it and instantly forgot to look for his identification.

There was a large stack of cash inside the wallet. I pulled out the bills and dropped the wallet. Quickly counting the money, I found it totaled up to $170. This meant I only needed another $80 to pay for the tests. I looked left and right, finding nothing more than an empty road bathed in the darkness of night.

I climbed back into my car and drove home, leaving his corpse in the road. I didn't know his reason for walking that street, and his loss wasn't my problem. When I got home, I took the bumper off of my car in case someone came asking questions. I put it in the back tool shed that contained our lawn equipment. I wasn't sure what I would do with it, but that was a problem for a different day. The first issue was finding the rest of the money I needed. I managed to go through my sister's room before she made it home and found the money she'd saved for her drugs—$20 more than I needed.

I ended up paying the school for the tests and used the remaining money on a pint of cheap vodka and pack of cigarettes to celebrate my inevitable success.

I thought about how appropriate it would be to have a private memorial to show my appreciation to the guy I'd hit with my car. Without his money, it would've taken considerably more effort to get what I needed. However, once my focus shifted to passing the tests, I didn't give him another thought. I momentarily considered what it meant that I had no massive response to what happened, then deciphered a method of obscuring my role with ease and celebrated how it benefited me. It was easier to digest these facts, as I had already accepted the shadow me as an inseparable aspect of my personality. Plus, I didn't know the man. I'd had more of a relationship with Gray and hadn't grieved his death at all either.

I passed each of the tests with minimal effort, gaining the credits necessary to leave the prison of high school. Still, I was forced to finish the school year so that I could participate in graduation, which I refused to attend.

My father had to work and wasn't going to be there. My mother got angry and told me, "You need to go. It's a big deal that I get to celebrate all the work I did to get you to graduation." It took more effort to withhold my laughter at her egocentric mentality and delusional recall than it did to graduate early.

I had already been accepted into a university to

begin my schooling. It was out of state, but luckily, I qualified for several scholarships due to my academic successes. I would still eventually need a job to help supplement my lifestyle, and that required figuring out a field I could work in without the risk of too much conflict. I needed a place to stay, and I assumed living in the dorm with a roommate was potentially a hazardous situation.

I got a decent-paying summer job picking up roadkill off the highway. It wasn't glamorous, but it paid well. No one wanted to do it, because it required sitting alone in a truck all day and handling dead animals. These things didn't bother me the slightest, so it was easy to work hard and save money.

I moved a couple of weeks before school was supposed to start. The school contacted me about my interest in living in the dorms, and I immediately rejected their offer. I knew that there would be a decent chance I would be forced to share a room with a person that I couldn't stand. I decided I found it preferable to live in my car for the first month or so, and during that time find a job and ensure I could support myself in an apartment by myself.

I found a job working in IT. It was extremely easy, once I understood how a computer system worked. It's easy to identify what could be causing potential issues. It also allowed for the majority of my social interactions to be conducted over the phone, which was helpful because I didn't have to exert energy on looking interested or concerned for the client's issues. I discovered that I could easily manage relationships with coworkers on a schedule. I was confident that I could maintain a level of small talk that would put those around me at ease while keeping a distance that ensured my comfort.

Living in my car wasn't horrible. There were truck stops that offered showers, and laundromats for my clothes. My diet was affected more than anything. I was forced to resort to eating junk food that didn't require cold for storage or heat to prepare. However, between what I made in the first couple paychecks at my new job and what I had saved back home picking up roadkill, I was able to save money for an apartment only a couple of weeks after school started.

I watched the other freshmen struggle to adjust to a life without family support and being tossed into an environment with little to no familiarity. The transition barely affected me because those obstacles reflected my existence up to that point. Classes were asinine and barely a step above the difficulty of high school, so much so that I coasted through my first semester as if I were sleepwalking.

I did realize that my original plan to completely isolate myself was somewhat flawed. Initially, the monotonous nature of my routine was helpful, but eventually it led to an increased urge for impulsive risk taking. I began having more one-night-only sexual encounters and drinking more alcohol. I knew I needed an outlet for my destructive side, which led me to joining a kendo dojo.

The Japanese art of the sword oddly complemented and reinforced how I was already navigating the world around me. You must learn the techniques and be capable of great violence, yet constantly exercise self-control to ensure that violence is only utilized in the most extreme situations. There was no requirement for meaningless pleasantries; everyone knew their role and didn't have to extend past it. There was just instructor and student, no perspective of a faux family that required appeasement. It was good, hard work. I dedicated most of my time to training when I wasn't already working or in school.

This was how my life went for a good deal of time. Until one person had to toss a rock that disrupted the tranquil waters I'd worked hard to tame.

6

GUILT AND SHAME

All people are capable of deceit, thievery, manipulation, and harm. As a matter of fact, at least one of the previously mentioned behaviors will inject itself into every relationship we experience throughout our lives. Even if it's lies of omission or unintended harm, it is inevitable. Accepting that fact allows us to better handle those situations as they occur. The most confusing part of the equation is the fact that so many people feel guilt and shame about it.

Guilt is the internally inspired emotion you experience when you feel you should have done more. You should've been more honest, or tried harder to help. Shame comes from external sources and typically stems from feeling like you should've done less. You shouldn't have gotten so drunk, or should have had sex with less people. I don't comprehend why these emotions are so commonly discussed or encouraged.

Why should I change who I am simply because another person was inconvenienced by my actions? I would also never tear myself down because somebody else told me I should have done more.

I have never actually experienced guilt, and I'm extremely grateful for that. I have watched too many people wrestle with it over the years, and it seems like a truly horrendous experience. I have experienced regret after having to manage some negative consequences of my actions. Regret and guilt are different though, because regret is focused on the action and guilt is focused on the individual that committed the action. I don't get mad at myself for doing something that I thought was a good idea. If I choose to lie, it is because I want to lie for a specific reason. That reason doesn't change even if hindsight provides me with a clearer understanding of how my dishonesty hurt someone. When I chose to start hurting people, it was because I wanted to do it. I've long thought that guilt holds people back from being truly authentic.

I don't feel guilty. I am built this way.

Guilt and shame are born from a fictitious belief that we can ever be perfect, that our actions will ever be able to fully align and conform to each individual's moral code. Whatever we do in our lives will negatively affect someone. This makes guilt unavoidable. Any person who makes decisions in order to avoid guilt or shame is living solely from fear. How can anyone ever be truly happy if there is a foundation of fear in all of their choices? Guilt played no role in my decisions. I only chose to show compassion to someone because I wanted to avoid near-certain consequences or because it conformed to the person I wanted to be.

Shame makes even less sense to me. At least guilt comes from intrinsic evaluation of your behaviors. I can't imagine what it is like to care so deeply about how others assess my choices that I would be put into a state of distress. Should I change the things that bring me joy to fit in with others better? Any reasonable person would say no. Shame is nothing more than an attempt to control others to fit into our own boxes.

The basic concept behind guilt and shame is that the desires of the other or of the group should outweigh the desires of the person experiencing the emotion. Why are you so deeply affected by other people's opinions? Do you value belonging to a group so strongly that you let their feelings and opinions impede who you are as a person?

There is also a perverse pleasure in manipulating another person using guilt or shame. I enjoy knowing that I can make a simple statement and give a disappointing stare, and others will fall into line.

My first few semesters of college went by relatively easily. I maintained my regular schedule of class, work, kendo, and random sexual encounters. The sex usually only occurred at most once a month, because that seemed to be the point where the lack of release caused me to become more irritable or aggressive. On a few occasions, one of the girls that I had gone home with would see me in public and attempt to confront me. They typically said the same things about how could I be so heartless, why would I lie, or just a series of obscenities about how mean I was. When those approaches didn't work, they would almost always resort to attacks against my physical endowment or sexual performance.

None of their attacks ever registered as bothersome enough to even respond to. These girls never meant anything to me, so their opinions and feelings meant nothing as well.

I went for quite a while without any risky behaviors, aggressive encounters, or physical harm caused. I was starting to find a way of living that allowed me to conduct myself and move about others without arousing any suspicion. Generally, classes were far too simple, but I did find my psychology courses extremely interesting. I got to learn about typical development and then compare it to my own developmental milestones. It was interesting to take an objective third-party view of myself and gain a greater understanding of how I became the person I was.

Sometimes this involved immersive conversations about difficult topics, such as trauma, abuse, etc. I was surprised to see how many of my peers became uncomfortable when a topic was approached that they related to personally. Their responses were defensive and argumentative, often aiming their ire directly at the professor or a student that had asked a fair question that stemmed from naivete. Honestly, I felt this was ridiculous. We all have adverse childhood experiences, so why would it bother them to hear about the general effects of those experiences? They had to live through them; they should have already been aware.

The most interesting thing I learned in my studies was that apparently, one of the criteria for the majority of mental health diagnoses was that it needed to cause a disruption in functioning. This concept made me question myself heavily. Up to that point in my life, my thoughts and behaviors had only caused minimal impairment in functioning. I had lost a job and engaged in occasional unnecessary and unintended conflict.

However, by my own evaluation, it was only a mild impairment. I was able to take care of myself, nurture the relationships I wanted (I wanted none), and succeed academically and occupationally as long as I properly considered my environment.

This further led me away from any desire to change or seek assistance. I began to rejoice in my differences and take pride in the fact that I wasn't like all of the people around me. If being mentally well meant being like those peers sitting in my classes, I gladly chose mental unwellness. Noticing an increased drive and motivation to push myself as I took pride in who I was, I decided I would take as many chances as possible to foster that sense of pride. I wanted to give myself tangible rewards for all of the hard work I was doing, and for the ability to manage my mental state as well as I was. I didn't want or need much, so the most logical option was to reward myself by going out and enjoying a nice dinner once every two weeks when I got paid. I allowed myself this treat as long as I hadn't engaged in any potentially risky behavior during those weeks.

There was a steakhouse that wasn't too far from my apartment. It was nice, and even though it was usually busy, there only ever seemed to be a short wait. As months passed, I became what the staff called a regular. They would greet me when I came in the door as if we were old friends. I put on a big enough smile so as not to be awkward or offensive, then requested a small booth that I could share with my own thoughts and nothing more. I usually ordered the same meal, because there is a certain amount of comfort that accompanies routine. I knew what I liked, and that was all I needed.

The other part of my routine was my server. She was a young woman, no more than a year older than me. She had long brown hair that she usually kept in a ponytail, and she was extremely attractive. Yet what caused her to stand out from all of the other women at the restaurant was that she didn't wear any makeup. She was being unashamedly herself, it seemed. She didn't need to wear the traditional face paint to hide her flaws and highlight her positive attributes; she just was who she was.

I didn't know how to interpret this completely. She also never displayed signs of being stressed, over-whelmed, or depressed; she was always put together in every other way, which meant it was just a choice.

I had considered trying to seduce her, but I knew I would have to find a new restaurant to frequent after the eventual fallout. That seemed like more trouble than the sex was actually worth. So, I continued my routine, and with each new visit, the waitress would so-cialize more with me and ask me how things were going. I would bring in books that I was reading from different philosophers or psychologists through history, and she would ask me about them. She seemed per-fectly pleasant and polite, but I assumed it was just a tactic to get a better tip from me. I didn't mind hon-estly, because she wasn't annoying or intrusive about it. I actually began requesting that she be my waitress every time I dined.

One Friday night, I was enjoying my usual order

when she walked up to the table to refill my drink. She paused for a minute and stared at me. I expected her to ask about the book I was reading, by Schopenhauer, but she took me by surprise.

"Why haven't you asked me out yet?" She stood there with a casual posture and genuine curiosity. There was no anger or irritation to be found.

I didn't know how to respond. I had spent so little time tinkering with my social mechanics that being caught off guard highlighted the rust that impeded my ability to react. "Um...I figured that was inappropriate. You're trying to work, and I didn't want to make you uncomfortable." It was always a safe bet to explain your actions as an attempt to protect the other person.

Her face twisted. She looked at me as if that was the dumbest answer I could've given. It wasn't a look of condescension or shame, just bewilderment. "So, you come in here every two weeks, sit at *my* table, talk to me and ask me questions, and you see that I spend at least twice as much time at your table than others. But that was all just my job and your respect for my job?"

What was she doing? I felt nervous, put on the spot. I had never had a relative stranger challenge me so directly. We didn't even have an actual relationship. I was a customer, and she was my server. I began rolling through my list of possible responses, but none of them seemed to fit this situation. This random woman was being the aggressor in this situation, and I felt like prey for the first time.

She became impatient. "Okay, so I am going to

request the Friday two weeks from now off, since that's when you go out. And you need to pick a restaurant, because I don't want to go on a date to my job. Then you are going to pick me up at seven, and we are going to go eat and have fun conversations. Any questions?"

Who did she think she was? No one gave me orders like this. She didn't say any of it aggressively. Just matter-of-factly, telling me what our plans were going to be. It particularly threw me for a loop that she took my schedule into consideration. She wasn't telling me to go out with her just because she wanted it; she wanted me to be comfortable also.

"Well," I said, "I haven't ever eaten at another restaurant in the area. So, I don't know what's good."

She looked puzzled again. "You've never gone to a different place to eat? Seriously? Okay, I'm going to check on my other tables. You decide if you want pizza, Italian, or sushi. When I come back, you tell me, and I'll decide the best place to go."

With that, she walked away. I watched her hips sway as she strutted to her next table. Her gait resembled that of the victor of a fight. She'd come to the table with an intention and walked away successfully. However, she did it with no manipulation or deception that I could detect.

I sat there for fifteen minutes, my book open in my hands but not reading. My mind was trying to process the interaction, and it just wasn't able to compute.

She came back over to the table eventually. "Well, what's the decision?"

I had my response ready this time. I confidently

looked at her and stated, "Sushi." I thought my simple answer would wrap up this moment so that I could go home and figure out what all had transpired. I was wrong.

"Nice choice. Why?" she asked, smiling.

"What do you mean why? I had an answer to your question."

"Yeah, and I appreciate it. But I want to make sure it's what you really want, and not just you giving a random answer."

This woman was odd—and now more than slightly irritating.

"I chose sushi because I didn't understand the difference between pizza and Italian. They're pretty similar. I chose the outlier."

She began laughing. Not at me, but a real laugh, like my statement was a joke. "You're a very confusing person, but I think you're interesting. Sushi it is. Here's my number. Call me Friday so we can set up the details." She handed me a piece of paper from her pocket with her number, refilled my water, laid down the check for the meal, and walked away.

I didn't even finish my meal. I was completely out of my element, and my mind was struggling to understand everything running through it. I pulled cash from my wallet and debated if I should leave the same tip as usual, or more, or less? I never debated myself. I always moved with certainty and confidence, but now I was questioning what tip amount would be offensive to this waitress I barely knew.

I went back home and decided that the best route for me would be to put her completely out of my mind.

There was no way for me to understand her fully, but going on this date would at least provide an opportunity for further understanding of socialization.

Two weeks passed by relatively normally. I was able to regain and maintain my focus by going to more of the kendo classes. I made the decision to have no plan going into the date. As much as she was able to take control of the situation in the restaurant, it wouldn't happen again. I had always been able to stay flexible and adjust to a situation, then use that to become the dominant party. Even if she was able to be that direct, now that I could expect it, I would be able to throw her off balance. She wouldn't have the advantage of being in her own environment, and that would most likely disrupt her comfort.

I called her an hour before seven, and she gave me her address. I said I would be there in about forty-five minutes.

I pulled up to her house five minutes after seven so that she would be slightly anxious about whether I was coming or not. I went to her door to get her, and when she opened it, I didn't offer any apology. Not that it mattered—she looked completely unfazed. She was wearing jeans and a T-shirt that slightly hugged her figure, but not enough that she was trying to show it off.

We rode to the restaurant in silence for the most part, other than a brief conversation about how our weeks were going. I asked if I could turn on some music so that I could focus on driving. I thought the question would be somewhat offensive to her, just enough to drain some of that confidence she had.

Instead, she agreed and immediately got excited at the album choice.

I always knew I was somewhat broken. I was comfortable and confident being the slightly defective toy that none of the kids wanted to play with. However, this girl seemed just as broken as me. Not in the same way, or at least not that I could tell, but she seemed completely unflappable. Her defects seemed to only be obvious in her interest in the defective toy.

We got to the restaurant and got a table. I ordered something that looked nice enough. I never gave much consideration to what I ate, because it was only for the purpose of sustenance. Once the waiter took our orders and walked away, she looked at me and asked, "So why psychiatry? I remember you telling me that's what you were wanting to go to school for, and it seems like a lot of work. You must be really passionate."

This seemed like a very odd way to start a conversation, and maybe a touch too personal. Social protocols typically dictated that conversations start with surface-level icebreakers and then gradually sink to more personal depths. I thought about it for a moment. "I don't think it's a passion. I think I would be good at it. People are all different, even though the internal parts are the same. I think that's interesting and wanted to work in the medical field."

"Fair. But why psychiatry? You could be a surgeon or nurse or any other job in the medical field, but you chose one with mental illness. I think that's neat."

What was with this girl's questions? I debated the level of honesty that I wanted to apply here. Usually,

I would've sold some story about being extremely compassionate and wanting to help those that are mis-understood, but that felt like the wrong play with this girl. "I think too many people in the mental health field are too compassionate. They see people with problems, and they have sympathy for them. So much sympathy that they hold back. I think that's a waste of time—and something I can change. A psychiatrist should see the patient as a combination of their re-ported symptoms, family history, and biological makeup, then prescribe medication and offer treat-ment to address the overall diagnosis."

This level of honesty was only slightly risky. I was being honest—I didn't feel sympathy for people—but I held back the level of disconnection I knew I would experience.

"So like a car mechanic? You see what's wrong and fix it. No need to feel bad for the car because its trans-mission is slipping, just deal with the problem and move on."

Understanding and acknowledgment. I nodded as I took a drink from my water.

"I think that's pretty cool," she continued. "I don't know much about mental health, but I'm guessing if a doctor cares too much, he might make excuses or miss something because it's scary. You want to be different. Helping people by not seeing them as people."

There was no judgment in her voice. I didn't know how to respond, so I sat there silently drinking my water. After a few moments of uncomfortable silence, the waiter brought food to the table. As I was preparing to eat, she spoke up again. "Okay, stop." She shoved both her hands in front of her as if attempting to will me not to eat.

She took a deep breath and looked straight into my eyes. There was no anger or irritation, but her look was serious and intense. "I think we both know how first dates are supposed to go. We're supposed to flirt a little, share just enough truth to make sure the other person stays interested while also keeping a distance so we don't seem needy or weird. I don't like to play games. So..." She took a pause here for just a moment. "I propose that we both take our masks off and just be ourselves. If it's a good fit, great. If it isn't, then I promise I won't spit in your food when you come to the restaurant."

My eyebrows furrowed as I considered what she'd just said. I'm sure she still to this day thinks that I was confused by her statements about necessary deception and masks, but that was far from it. My mask doesn't come off. It is a permanent fixture that remains attached at all times, except in my inner dialogue. This is purposeful and intentional. It is to protect me from being exposed. Now, this woman was sitting across from me asking me to remove it completely so she could see the real me. My guard was instantly raised, and I felt like a wolf watching another predator trying to encroach on my territory.

"Give me an example," I said cautiously. I wanted to see how truthful she would be and how open to her own idea she was.

Her eyes went up and to the side as she considered what she'd say next. "Fair—I'm asking you to be completely honest, so you want proof I will be also. First off, I hate dating. I hate having to look nice but not too nice so the guy isn't threatened or insecure. Why can't I go on a date in pajama pants? Why do I have to laugh at jokes that are bad? And how much should I worry that the guy sitting across from me is some deranged pervert who wants to keep me in his basement? I'm not saying you are, but that's what I was told as a woman. Be careful of creeps." She expelled the entire rant in one breath, like she was divulging some guilty secret that she desperately needed to release.

I digested her comment. As I sat there and rolled it around in my mind, I started to chuckle. She looked a bit offended. "Don't laugh at me. That is a real thought."

My chuckling faded away. "I'm not laughing at you. It was just kind of cute. Your big confession that you were hiding behind your mask was that you wanted to wear pajamas tonight."

"Okay, so what do you have, Mr. Mystery? You share something that you wouldn't dare share on a first date."

I contemplated her challenge. I felt like I could say almost anything. She seemed more down to earth than anyone I'd ever met. Even with this sense of security, though, my innate urge to protect myself kept me from going too far. "Well first, I have no interest in keeping you in my basement. And not just because I don't have a basement. But if I had to choose one thing to share...I would tell you that this is the first date I've been on since I was maybe fifteen years old. Depending on what you call a date."

Her jaw hit the table. "You're kidding. So you haven't been in a relationship in years?" She back-pedaled a bit, probably recognizing the shock in her voice. "I'm not judging, but why?"

I answered without hesitation. "I don't like most people. I get irritated quickly and feel like it's too much work to protect their feelings. It's easier to stay to my-self. I don't have to wear a mask. I don't have to pre-tend I care more than I do. I can just enjoy my peaceful life. So far, every time someone interrupts that peace, my entire life is turned upside down. Maybe not at first, but eventually."

I studied her face as I spoke, and all I could see was a genuine interest. There was no look of disapproval. She didn't think I was a freak. I paused before adding, "But I am glad that you asked me out here tonight."

Her cheeks flushed red, and her lips turned up into a bashful smile. I wasn't lying or manipulating her with that statement, and she was enjoying my company. She looked to the side and coyly asked, "So what's the other reason you aren't going to kidnap me if it's not just that you don't have a basement? Am I not good kidnap material?"

I smirked at her obvious tease. "It also seems like way too much work to keep someone for that long."

We both laughed.

•   •   •

After some reflection, I was able to understand how she was able to get me to go out on that date with her and have such a good time. It was an impressive tactic, whether it was intentional or not. She was able to put me into a vulnerable state by taking me off guard and being so direct. Then, by allowing me to make a decision and being supportive and nonjudgmental, she was able to turn that vulnerable state into a more secure state. It was almost a predatory approach to maintaining a sense of control over another person. I was thoroughly impressed by this woman.

After that first date, I found an odd attraction to the waitress that I couldn't explain. I was never completely honest about myself, because I wasn't that foolish. However, I did find myself behaving differently than in past relationships. I would think about her when she wasn't around, and put in effort to spend more time together. We couldn't have been more different from each other. She had large groups of friends she would always ask if she could introduce me to, and each time I would find a reason to escape that dreaded social engagement. She studied acting and theater because she thought she could make the world a better place by bringing joy to others. She was goal oriented because of a deep-seated passion to help, whereas my goals always developed from what would best serve me. She spoke to her family often, and she would ask why I never spoke with mine. I don't know if I was hiding the truth about those aspects of my personality because I wanted to manipulate her because I wanted to protect myself from her seeing the cracks in my foundation.

She brought out a side of me that I didn't know existed. I was actually enjoying the company of another person. She always had something on her mind and loved talking about it. She would talk for hours about the difference between comedy and drama, how theater was superior to film, or how she thought that tipping culture was implemented poorly. I started to realize I actually enjoyed listening to her talk about her interests. I didn't find the topics all that interesting, but seeing a person so comfortable being unapologetically passionate about an uncommon passion was relieving. I even started to be more comfortable with nonsexual displays of physical affection. It wasn't extremely comfortable, but I think she was the first person with whom I allowed myself to cuddle. When she would ask about things I wanted to keep hidden, I wouldn't outright lie. Instead, I chose a tactic of changing the subject.

We of course introduced sex into our dynamic within the first couple of weeks, but even with that, it never felt like I was using her to get the climax I wanted. That was the first issue I had in our relationship. I enjoyed sex where I could use the other person without any consideration of their thoughts and feelings. There was a level of intimacy here that prevented me from doing this.

The most logical solution to the problem was for me to continue my previously established sexual behavior behind her back. Once every couple of months, I would still go out and find a girl in a store, flirt with her and manipulate her into bed, then abandon her completely. It was similar to taking medication. My mind needed the act of physical and mental dominance over another person, so I found opportunities without involving the waitress.

One day, several months into our relationship, she reached out to me and continued the same conversation about me meeting her friends. I wanted to get out of it, but she managed to convince me that it would just be one lunch out in public and I was welcome to leave whenever I wanted. I think she felt I was nervous about what they would say to me, but the reality was I just didn't want to have to talk to that many people. I agreed because it seemed important to her, and I wanted to try to put forth more effort. It seemed like a fair trade-off for me continuing to have sex with other people.

The lunch went decently enough for a group social activity. Her friends were far less remarkable than she was, but I managed to be polite with everyone. A few of her friends seemed very standoffish with me from the moment of my arrival; I paid them no mind and gave them the same effort that they gave to me.

One of her male friends seemed far too forward with me. He was slightly taller but had a considerably smaller frame than me. It was obvious that he had some form of romantic feelings toward the waitress. Every question he directed at me would transition into a competition between the two of us. He made passive-aggressive comments about being very protective of her. He even went so far as to tell me that he "would really mess up anyone who hurt her."

I found his approach laughable. His attempts to

intimidate me were completely unsuccessful. They didn't even work to irritate me, because I knew I was the one that she had chosen.

The lunch finished, and the waitress told me that she and her female friends were going to have a girls' night together. I told her to have fun and went back to my apartment. I read for a while as the hours passed into the evening, and as dinner time came, I decided to watch a movie.

Partway through the movie, my phone began to ring. I looked at the caller ID, and it was the waitress.

"Hello," I said. "How's it going?"

Her tone came across curt and direct. "I need to ask you a question. Do you have a moment?"

My guard went up immediately. I knew this conversation wasn't going to go well, but I figured there might be a way to maneuver my way out of incoming accusations that were unsubstantiated. "Yes. I'm just at home. What is going on?"

"So, two of my friends that you met today told me that you slept with them both and never called them back. I know you haven't really talked about your past relationships much, and I didn't ask who all you've had sex with, but I think it's pretty messed up that you didn't feel the need to tell me that you were going around screwing people and abandoning them." She didn't hide her anger. She felt betrayed and wanted to make sure I knew.

No guilt swelled in my chest. No regret occupied my mind. I couldn't remember the girls, and I didn't know if I had slept with them before I met the waitress or after.

Still, I knew I had to play this carefully. "I apologize. I didn't recognize them during lunch because I was meeting so many people, and it was overwhelming. If I had, I would've said something to you first. I can tell you're hurt, but I don't know what to say right now."

I could hear her take a deep breath, and with a still agitated tone she asked, "How many people did you sleep with before we got together?"

Small victory. I could easily navigate this, since it was before our relationship. "I honestly don't know. I told you I haven't been good at dating, so that's all I ever really looked for."

There was a long silence on the phone before she responded. Her voice was calmer this time, but there was still a level of intensity. "Thank you for being honest. I'm still hurt because it shocked me. I just need to think a bit about this."

I acknowledged what she'd said, and we hung up. I sat in silence for a few minutes, considering the different outcomes. I would be fine if she left, even though a part of me didn't want her to. She wasn't just direct and assertive, she also was not judging me at all. Even hearing about my past, she only spoke about her hurt. She didn't say anything about me. She was unique compared to everyone else.

I returned to my movie, accepting that there was nothing else I could do at this point. I had to let her simmer in what had happened. I knew that my calm and "honest" directness would win some bonus points in the situation, considering these friends that told her about me were probably angry and spiteful. Their excessive emotion would make me look more grounded. I began to consider that maybe I should stop having sex with other girls, but I knew that I wasn't motivated enough for that.

I watched a second movie, just in case she decided to call back. She didn't. However, toward the end of the film, I received a text from an unknown number. I looked down, and it read, *I told you that you'd regret hurting her. Thanks for giving me the go ahead with her.*

I knew who it was. It was the douchebag from lunch earlier that day, her friend that obviously was attracted to her. I didn't know if the first sentence was intended to be a threat or not. It didn't scare me or make me angry, but I was deeply offended that this boy thought he had the right to confront me as if he was superior. I took a few deep breaths and decided not to act until I heard back from the waitress. There would be no reason to not confront him about the perceived threat if she ended things with me. However, me beating up her friend would only make things worse if she considered staying.

I took a shower and went to bed. It was difficult at first, because my thoughts began to get away from me. I imagined beating the douchebag with my bare hands, envisioned stabbing him in the throat. I only knew that I fell asleep because I was woken by my phone ringing. I looked at the clock and saw that it was 3 a.m. and the waitress was calling me. I wiped the sleep from my eyes and gathered myself enough to answer the phone.

"Hey. It's really late, are you okay?"

Her voice sounded less angry and less intense

now. "I'm sorry for waking you up. I'm a little drunk and I didn't want to wait for morning to talk to you." I immediately recognized that this could go in either direction. Alcohol makes people erratic and unpredictable, and I don't enjoy not being able to make predictions. It's harder to control the situation, so I needed to proceed cautiously.

"You're good. What did you need to talk about?"

"I'm sorry about calling you earlier. It wasn't fair for me to put you on the spot and be mad about something that happened before we even met. I got really jealous when they said they had slept with you and then scared that you would leave me without any conversation like you did with them. But you haven't, and that was silly." I could tell she was crying slightly. It seemed like the alcohol in her system was working in my favor. Instead of holding on to anger, she was feeling guilty about being rude to me. I could use this in my favor in the future.

"It's okay. We can't always control our reactions. I appreciate you calling, but you should get some sleep." Be the forgiving and dutiful boyfriend, check. Care about her well-being when she feels guilty about how she treated me, check. This was lining up too perfectly, but I knew I could ensure that this conversation wouldn't happen again. "But before you go, I have a question for you. That guy friend of yours from lunch texted me. It sounded like he was with you or something. Should I be worried?"

Truth was, I wasn't worried at all. I wanted to see if I could instigate more guilt so that, in the future, she would second-guess confronting me about fidelity. If I could make her feel more guilty, then she would do anything to avoid repeating this process a second time.

Her voice shifted again and became extremely irritated, with a hint of spite. "Yeah, screw him. He's an asshole. He called one of the other girls, who told him what was going on. I guess she got into my phone and gave him your number. Then he called me, and I thought I could trust him. So, I told him how I was feeling, and we hung up. Then, this son of a bitch started texting me to try and hook up. What a creep."

This was my chance. Her anger had transitioned to another target, one that she viewed as careless and emotionally immature. "Well, I appreciate you telling me. It kind of hurts that I had to ask about it, instead of finding out from him and then talking to you. I'll be okay. I just need some time to process it." I did my best to replicate her behavior from earlier to drive home that betrayal can go both ways.

Her voice shifted again. This time, the guilt was pouring from her in thick waves like from a ruptured syrup bottle. "I'm so sorry. I didn't want to upset you. But you're right. That's all my fault. Please don't be mad at me." I let silence hang on the phone for a moment. A silence she broke. "But you did give me space when I needed it. I'll do the same. I'm really sorry. I love you."

I was taken aback by that last statement. She'd just drunkenly confessed that she loved me. "I love you too. Goodnight." I had no other response, but I knew that was the easiest way to end that conversation.

I lay in the darkness of my room, processing yet an-other conversation. She loved me? How odd. She barely knew me. I knew that this situation would easily be swept under the rug, partially because of her guilt and partially her embarrassment at her confessions. It still gave me an uncomfortable sensation. She loved me. My first response was to feel like it was gross. Oddly, that feeling was quickly replaced by some kind of satisfaction. It felt nice that she cared.

I felt comfortable with how I'd handled everything, until my thoughts started to stray to the douchebag. I expected one of two responses to the situation: com-plete indifference or the same hot rage I had felt in the past. I was wrong. As I thought about him texting her, using my mistake as a means of taking advantage of her, my body experienced another new sensation.

With the rage in the past, it was as if a furnace in my stomach began to spew fire to my face, hands, and legs. My whole body would burn. This time, it was like there was ice running through my entire network of veins. I felt cold, angry, and determined.

I didn't sleep that night. I lay in that bed and thought of my plan.

The next few weeks went by flawlessly. The wait-ress and I moved past the awkwardness of that night and didn't speak about it again. She put forth more effort into respecting my lack of desire to be around her friends, even to the point of no longer asking. We both started saying that we loved each other more. I agreed to do it, because I had said it that one night on the phone and I didn't see any harm from it. I didn't understand what the word meant or how she could possibly feel it toward me, but I didn't argue.

I took the information I knew about her douchebag friend and decided that I would learn more about him. He had let slip where he worked during the one conversation we had. So, about two weeks after that night, I skipped class and called out of work. I sat outside his job for several hours just to watch. I saw him leave the building and get in his car. I followed him home and noted where he lived in my head. It was a decent enough one-story house. It made no sense how he could afford a house in his twenties, but I didn't give it much further thought. I stayed there the entire night and watched for when he left for work again.

I did this maybe two or three times a week for the following month. He worked in a tattoo shop at the time, and it seemed like his hours were irregular, but he never came home before 1 a.m. Sometimes he would leave work and go straight home, sometimes he would go to a bar, but still never home before one. The time he left for work was much more consistent: 3:30 p.m.

I had my plan, I knew his address, and I knew his schedule. At the end of the month following him, I spoke with the waitress and said that I had tests coming up and wanted to try to get more sleep. She said she understood, and we agreed not to hang out that night. I found out there was a way to schedule a text message to send at a specific date and time. I turned off my lights and climbed into bed at about 9 p.m. and took a photo of myself looking sleepy with the caption *Love you and miss you*. I scheduled that text to be sent at midnight.

The ice in my system had never thawed. I was angry the entire time I followed him, the entire time I was getting closer with her. I would not let it go that this boy thought it wise to threaten me, disrespect me, and make my girlfriend uncomfortable. I got up after taking the picture and got dressed in black clothing so I wouldn't be seen. I gathered the items I had bought over the last several weeks and put them in the trunk of my car.

After leaving the house, I stopped to get some fast food. I'd found during my nights watching him that I became extremely hungry when I wasn't sleeping well. I had always been on a consistent sleep schedule, so this was new to me.

I pulled up at his house sometime around 11:30 p.m. The windows in the neighborhood were completely dark. I parked several houses down from his and walked to his yard. The five-gallon can of gasoline I was carrying was awkward in my arm and throwing my balance off.

My plan was simple. Pour gas on his back porch, light it. Pour gas on his front porch, light it. Then, return to my car and let his bungalow-style house burn to its own content. I didn't think beforehand that I would be lucky enough that this fool would leave a window open.

It was too high for me to climb through, so I poured almost half the contents of my can into the window and threw in a match, then continued to the back porch. With being able to start a fire indoors, I thought the front porch would be an unnecessary risk. I moved quickly, but with purpose and intention. I didn't want to stay long enough that any neighbors waking up would potentially see me. From the moment that I threw the first match into the window to the back porch catching fire was maybe a minute.

I rushed back to my car, carrying the empty gas can. I knew the fire had started, and I didn't care enough to sit around and watch it burn. I didn't want to hurt the boy, but I did want him to suffer some. He intruded on my property by trying to sleep with my girlfriend and betraying her trust, so I invaded his property with gas and matches.

I left the gas can in my garbage and put bags of trash over it. There was no actual forensic evidence that could tie the can to his house if the police were even able to connect the fire to me. I had made no threatening statements to or about him. No one had seen me angry. I had an alibi in the text message that had been sent automatically at midnight.

I don't know if the waitress ever spoke with him again, but I'm sure she eventually found out what happened. She and I never spoke about him or the fire, though we actually saw him again a little less than a decade after. My wife and I were getting coffee when she saw him. They caught up like old friends, the awkward sexual advance forgotten. He was working in construction and looked like the years hadn't been kind to him. When she asked him what happened to his dreams of being a tattoo artist, he hung his head low.

"Yeah. I gave up on that. Remember when we used to hang out, but then we stopped?" A look of shame flashed across his face. "Well, there was a fire one night, and my parents didn't get out of the house in time. I had to find a new place to stay and deal with all of the funeral stuff. I kind of had to give up on that dream while dealing with everything."

I remember what I thought as I listened to him. *That was how he could afford a house. He lived with his parents. I guess I never did see the house during the normal hours people come and go. That makes more sense now.*

8

MORALITY

People have an unexplainable and completely pointless compulsion to classify different activities or other people as either right or wrong. They receive some kind of false security by sorting the world into an overly simplified, dichotomous system. I've always assumed it is because people are cowardly or foolish and need an easy method of understanding their environment. Things are actually far more complicated, though. I don't understand how any single action with almost infinite effects can be so easily defined.

This dichotomous perspective is the root of morality. Morality defines the rules or principles by which we differentiate between good and bad. All cultures have had different ways to do this, but the primary method has been religion. Religions set forth a list of rules for all followers to obey should they hope to receive whatever magnificent rewards are promised by their faith. At times, society will supplement these overarching rules with specific moral guidelines that address specific groups within the culture, often self-contradictory. For example, Christians have the testament that thou shalt not kill. Then, during the crusades, the knights who fought against the "evil heathens" must have been spared punishment for breaking that rule because of their role in the military.

What's important is this: if every culture has formed differing sets of rules, then that means that morality is subjective. If morality is subjective, then that means that there isn't truly a good or bad. The system of black-and-white thinking nurtured throughout human history is a complete lie to help the meek and defenseless sleep at night.

Take lying. Is lying for personal gain bad? Is lying about Santa's existence bad? Is lying to your pastor bad? To your teacher? To your parents? To yourself? The question can be altered in miniscule ways that potentially change the answer. Morality is completely subject to situation and intent.

Is murder evil? I mean the purposeful and intentional decision to end another person's life for any reason outside of self-defense or compassion (such as assisted suicide for those that are fatally ill).

I have read numerous posts by typical red-blooded Americans about the need to publicly murder pedophiles, regardless of if they served their time in prison. Sometimes the method of death is graphic and extreme. Socially acceptable evil.

How is the death sentence any better? Take a criminal and lock them in a cell; they no longer pose any threat to society. The death sentence serves as an act of retribution or vengeance on behalf of the victims. How is that not personal gain?

Morality shouldn't attempt to define behaviors; it should evaluate intentions. In every example I can think of, there are justifiable motivations to commit an act. A sex offender being killed because of something he did ten years ago because it bothers someone is not the same as a sex offender actively pursuing a victim being killed to protect that victim. Intention matters more than behavior.

I kill only those that I deem as fitting, and provide them every opportunity to stop me or escape from me, because I think that is fair. Stripping them of their ability to save themselves would only serve to gratify my desires by robbing them of their autonomy. I want to kill because I think a person is a drain on existence; they want to save themselves for self-preservation. Both are understandable desires and intentions. Then, we compete to see who will come out the victor.

Everything should be done with intention and forethought. Anything that is not is a mistake and should be corrected for moving forward. I used my mistake with the fire to ensure that only a desired target would fall prey to my actions after that. I didn't change my intention or my behavior. I accounted for possible ripple effects that don't align with my intention. If I recognized that I had a system that would stop me from accidentally harming a person again, and made the conscious decision to not use that system, I would be intentionally choosing to lose control. That would be bad.

I don't have the benefit of finding some obscure justification for my actions. I also don't think it is necessary to have one. I enjoy what I do, so I do it. Human beings are animals. Animals fight, steal, and kill for personal gain. At what point should I have concluded that I was better than any other animal? The urge is there. The control of the urge is there. I don't define my actions as evil because I don't think any of us are better than animals.

By almost all existing codes of right versus wrong, I am an evil person. Yet I've only ever met a handful of people whose selfishness, aggression, egocentrism, or constant deceit don't place them closer to me than they are to whatever their image is of morally righteous.

After the fire, my life began to take a turn. I had a great number of things to consider. I don't know if I would qualify the action I took as jealousy. It seemed more like possessiveness, another feeling I was very unfamiliar with. I had never cared about anyone enough to even view them as my possession, but the waitress was different. She had been different from the moment I met her, and she continued to prove herself different each day. After the fire was no different. She had forgiven me for her baseless accusations about my past and promised to only focus on the present and the future. Her faith in her friends began to waver, and she relied more heavily on me as her primary source of social support.

Recognizing that I viewed this woman as mine, I acted accordingly. I gave her what she needed to be happy while also protecting myself from becoming too close to her. I recognized that the darker half of me, which I had always attributed to heightened anger and aggression, was something much deeper. It was not just a heightened emotional response to threats. It was like an animal aspect of my mind that could easily over-power my more rational and logical self. A true Mr. Hyde to my everyday Dr. Jekyll, operating solely on base desire and violence. This realization was initially distressing, because it meant that there was a part of me that I might not ever fully control. I had dedicated so much effort to creating an environment to ensure no stimulus would pose a threat, and therefore nothing would require my reaction. I started to accept that maybe no amount of preparation would be sufficient.

I didn't see my compulsion for violence as an addic-tion. I never felt like I craved it. I also never saw it as some external person to myself. It was a part of me that I hid. It was the unsightly birthmark that I covered with clothing. No matter how close the waitress got, she would not be allowed a glimpse.

Outside of the relationship, my life progressed as I expected. Martial arts continued to become easier for me, and I began to compete in tournaments against other fighters outside of my own dojo. I won't say I was a natural, and my record was not perfect, but my finely crafted sense of control and comfort with aggression made the sport easier for me than for others. I could tell when an opponent had to overcome a natural empa-thy that stopped them from wanting to hurt someone. They would hesitate; I would not.

I was accepted into medical school at a prestigious university in the area. This was completely expected, as my GPA was perfect and none of my professors had a negative statement to make against me. My ability to understand and analyze people's psychology was well honed during my younger years, so schooling only required learning the terminology and anatomy.

Since my medical school was only about an hour away from where I received my bachelor's degree, I could stay where I was living. This was a calculated decision. I assumed that moving to another area would require too much of an adjustment of my day-to-day routine.

The waitress and I continued dating. She eventually stopped working at the restaurant and got a job working in a theater as some sort of stagehand; I can't remember the job specifically. She seemed to enjoy the job a lot, because it was closer to her passions. She distanced herself from the friends she had when we first met and started to make more friends at the theater. Luckily, she didn't push this time to have me meet any of them. I wasn't sure if it was because she knew that I wasn't interested or she was worried that another previous sexual conquest might be among them.

Her job did make planning time together extremely difficult because her schedule was so complicated. She still lived with her parents to save money, but they made late-night visits nearly impossible. I struggled with the inconsistency and what it did to my overall routine. She struggled because she missed me, which she reminded me of frequently. I didn't know how to respond to her when she said it, though. I enjoyed our time together, but I didn't ever experience a strong urge to see her; I also enjoyed my time by myself.

We were speaking on the phone one night during one of her breaks at work. She was tired and obviously upset because we hadn't seen each other in more than a week. I did my duty and showed empathy and understanding for her strife. I could hear that she was extremely sad, and I was becoming frustrated because I didn't know how to end these conversations once and for all.

I sat in silence on the phone before responding with the most logical solution. "Why don't you move in with me? We could see each other whenever you have free time, and you wouldn't have to be sad about this anymore."

She was overjoyed at my offer. She accepted and thanked me for taking things to the next stage in our relationship. I didn't understand fully, as she described me as being sweet and considerate. I'd simply offered the most rational solution to a problem I was tired of hearing about. I didn't think that having her there would impede my alone time much because she already worked so often. The added benefit of having someone to help with the bills was nice as well.

Over the next week, we started moving her belongings into my place.

My peers in graduate school began to pose a unique obstacle for me. The majority of them were the overly compassionate bleeding-heart types that you'd expect to go into the medical field. Their nauseating care for strangers seemed fake and forced. Many of them would discuss their own physical and mental health challenges, and it became apparent that they were in this field to scrape away at some invisible emotional scar tissue that they hadn't addressed directly. The professors ate it up, praising the wannabe saints for their unconditional, self-serving love. My respect for peers and professors alike eroded to disappointment, then disinterest, then disdain.

The schedule was challenging. The work was constant. The toll on my lifestyle was inevitable. The first crack appeared in one of my classes.

I was in my abnormal psychology lesson and we were discussing typical brain chemistry differences in people with severe diagnoses or personality disorders. We were split into groups of about eight people, with each group sitting around a circular table. These classes were annoying to me, because the seating was designed to promote conversation among students. I never fully adapted to this method of instruction. I knew I couldn't tell people that they were stupid outright, so I normally kept quiet and participated enough to maintain a high grade.

I found personality disorders to be extremely interesting, partially because I had one. However, there were also interesting differences between various disorders that could only be noticed with a true understanding of the person. Someone with antisocial personality disorder can absolutely appear narcissistic, and the same in reverse with someone that has narcissistic personality disorders. The biggest difference is the underlying drive and motivation. I was no narcissist, because I didn't have an inflated ego that needed to be paraded around and recognized by others. I didn't want people to see me as grandiose; I wanted them to leave me alone.

The creation of a personality disorder was like a mathematical equation in physics: a series of factors that must add together in the correct way, and when they do, they can explain the universe. That was not how my peers saw it, though. In this class, we discussed how those afflicted with such disorders treated the people around them, and what they hoped to achieve in those interactions. The class often became irritated by the manner in which the professor spoke. She presented everything as she should: pure fact with no bias or judgment.

Once the discussion began, the ignorant vultures that I had to call my peers swarmed the professor. One girl specifically spoke in an outraged tone that betrayed her hidden exposure to such treatment. It was clear through her word choices and tone that she had some negative encounter with a person that struggled with these disorders. I later discovered in a different class that she had dated a narcissist, and he was apparently abusive.

Regardless of her experiences, I couldn't stand that girl. She was the type who wanted to advocate for every oppressed group, because she viewed them as broken baby animals that needed tending. It was obnoxious and pitiful. I normally didn't respond, especially to her. I didn't see any purpose in conflict with people that refused to listen or learn. However, on this day, her voice was like nails on a chalkboard.

The specific conversation focused on reporting people that have violent urges or might be aggressive. She was going off on her rant to the professor, so the entire class quit their individual group conversations to listen. "We should be able to report anyone that might cause harm. I've dealt with someone who was diagnosed narcissistic, and he had no interest in changing. If someone could be causing harm to others, and refuses to change, isn't it our obligation to report them?" Her statements weren't completely unfounded. I wasn't aware of the effects of the fire I'd set yet, but I knew better than anyone the danger I posed and the desires I had experienced. However, it irked me to hear it in such an ignorant way.

I watched as the professor prepared to deliver another lecture about how our ethics outline reporting and imminent danger. As surprising to me as it was to the professor, I spoke up first. "What kind of harm? Just because someone has a disorder doesn't mean they're going to attack people."

The girl turned her attention from the professor to me. "Any kind? Harm is harm."

I leaned forward and placed my elbows on my knees. I felt an urge to challenge what she was saying. I wasn't positive if it was an innate urge to show her that she was mistaken, or I felt indirectly attacked by her comments. "Well, harm isn't always equal. A spouse who physically abuses his wife is doing harm. A parent who calls their child a piece of shit is also doing harm. They aren't equal."

She scrunched up her face as I spoke. I could feel

the condescension in her attitude from across the room. "As I said, it is our job to protect people, so it shouldn't matter what kind of harm. We should be allowed to report it."

I thought about it for a second, but I couldn't let it go. She was insinuating that a person should be reported because of what they are capable of, not what they have intent to do. "That seems to be a pretty ignorant viewpoint, in my opinion. Our job is supposed to be to help people. The people that come to us and ask for help. What gives any of us the right to decide someone deserves less than our full effort just because we don't like how they think?" The students at the other tables turned to face me. The professor looked at me, surprised but not displeased. She turned toward the girl, most likely hoping for a healthy and productive debate between students.

I had seen the glare she shot me too many times in my life at this point. Frustration with a dash of shock. She felt my challenge and had no good response. I felt the surge of excitement at having her into a corner and continued, "Besides, we already know these disorders are usually a ripple effect of trauma. Granted, it isn't the more comfortable timid response of cowering in your apartment, afraid of the world. But just because we find the fearful response more comfortable and favorable, we don't have the right to rank one over another." I intentionally used the word "we" to reduce the potential for her feeling attacked and getting more defensive.

The rest of the class fell quiet. The professor didn't interject. I had phrased my response respectfully, so there was no need for mediation yet. Later, she would tell me she let it continue because she thought that it would be a productive debate and she should've stopped it before it got out of hand.

The student scanned the room to see if anyone would defend her stance, but no one spoke up. "It's not the same. We are also required to protect people from harm. And some of these people actively fantasize about harming others. How do you propose we protect people while empathizing with the dangerous ones?" She flashed a smile filled with smug self-satisfaction.

A few students started to speak up at this point, convinced by the argument that spoke to their overly sympathetic nature. I realized that this was a losing fight. I didn't have faith in my ability to convince others that their job was not to save the world. I shook my head and leaned back in my seat, resigning myself to my previously cherished role as "quiet kid in class."

The professor locked eyes with me. I didn't have any issues with her usually. She respected that I didn't speak much and rarely disclosed my own experiences. She approached everything as logically as possible, and she seemed to have a lot of experience. The class looked from the girl, to me, and then carried on their group conversations about the situations in which they thought it was necessary to report someone. The professor spoke to me, loud enough that her voice overshadowed the class. "Are you done? It looks like you have something else you want to say." Her voice invited me to speak. She seemed to want to nurture the productive conflict between peers.

I sat up and faced the girl. I was speaking to the class but aimed the words at her. "It isn't our job to protect someone from ever getting their feelings hurt. We report someone to protect people that are in life-threatening and imminent danger. If someone chooses to stay in a verbally abusive relationship, that's their choice. We don't wear capes to work." There were a few muffled murmurs in the class before I continued. "Besides, you are talking about reporting a person after making an assumption about what they are going to do. Fantasies do not indicate intent to act. I can fantasize about eating ice cream but choose salad. Maybe our job should be to help whoever is sitting across from us until we *know* that they plan to act on the fantasy. Reporting them prematurely only increases the chance that they won't seek help later."

The professor looked satisfied with my response. I knew everything I said aligned with the ethics of our field. My words did incorporate a certain amount of sarcasm, but not enough to be a personal attack.

The self-righteous girl looked puzzled. "So, even if someone is mistreating people and making no progress, we should just keep trying? That's your opinion?"

"In order for you to see them, and potentially hospitalize them, they have to come into your office. It is a fair assumption that they want some change if they are there and paying to be there. If you are saying that there's no point in trying to treat them because they have fantasies, you're saying that psychiatry and therapy are ineffective. You should only report someone if they have the intention to lethally harm themselves or others." Now I replaced the royal we with a more direct "you."

This took her longer to respond to. A few other students allowed themselves to vocalize their support for her or me, but I paid them no attention. She was my target, and my focus was not so easily shaken. It was like we were standing on the mats at my dojo, trading blows, and the last statement I made was a kick that connected with her head. She was shook.

She eventually settled herself and recovered her composure. "I do think that what we do helps people. I also think that our job is to read people, and we can make educated assumptions to what people will do. If you had any experience with personality disorders, you'd know that these people aren't like other people. It's why they don't typically have friends, or families, or any other healthy relationships. They don't act like people, and most don't want to."

This was the right hook to my jaw. Her statement rang through my system. I was reminded of all the people that looked down on me and talked to me like I was less than human. I felt the furnace spread the heat of anger throughout my body. There was no chill, no cold and controlled rage. I picked up my textbook and slammed it onto the table I was seated at, then slid it across the table and knocked my bag, paper, and pencils onto the floor. The entire room froze and instinctively leaned away from me. All eyes were on me. I wasn't used to being the center of attention, so it was an uncomfortable sensation.

I looked the girl in her eyes. "Did you make an

educated guess that I would do that? No? Then maybe you aren't as omnipotent as you think." I stood up and gathered my items off the floor and left class. I didn't look at the professor or the other students as I left. The heat dissipated from me. The reality of my loss of control in such a public venue set in. I was somewhat scared of what I had done. I hadn't harmed anyone, but I also hadn't chosen my action intentionally. It was a reflex to a perceived threat. I dedicated so much time to controlling myself, and a snarky and arrogant girl had broken through that control with her ignorant statements.

The next day, my professor called me and asked me to come to her office. I was able to excuse my actions by providing a sob story about my friend who was hospitalized by a therapist because he admitted to having thoughts of harming himself, even though he didn't ever plan to act on them. I followed that up by stating that now he refuses to go back to therapy. It was a farce, but one based on stories I had heard from other people. She said she understood and let me go with a lecture about professional behavior in the workplace and classroom.

In truth, part of why it happened was that my mind was elsewhere, on other stressors. For about a month before that day, I'd been feeling conflicted about my relationship with the waitress. She had continued to be the thorn in my paw. She never seemed to judge me. She communicated with me and was open about her feelings, while showing an equal interest in mine. I was regularly having to dig deeper into my inner self to have genuine responses to her inquiries. She was attempting to remove pieces of my armor to see the scars she could tell I was hiding. The more confusing part was that I was letting her.

She was still working in the theater and had proven herself enough to be an assistant stage manager. She was spending more time with friends whenever she could. But every night she would show up back home, happy to see me. She took an interest in how my classes were going. When I told her about the argument in class, she told me how ridiculous the other girl was. She encouraged me to quit my job in the IT company and get a job in a hospital to start getting experience in the field I was working toward. Our lives were progressing, but she put forth an unexpected amount of effort to ensure they progressed together.

I'm not sure when it happened, but I began to feel safe and secure with her. More of the time I should've dedicated to my studies or training was being sacrificed to being with her. I even became fairly comfortable with physical contact with her. She challenged me in a way that I enjoyed, because it wasn't in any attempt to be superior. She defended me and was patient with me. She was the antithesis of everything I had learned about people.

I hated it. I hated every affection-filled moment. I couldn't grasp the concept of a person that genuinely cared for me for selfless reasons. We had been dating for over three years now, living together for almost a year. I knew I needed to change something, and after losing my control in class, I settled on my course of action.

My preparations were similar to those for the fire. I gathered information about the best avenue of approach. I gathered necessary materials. I waited a couple of months until the theater near me was doing a special showing of the first movie she and I had watched together, *Saw 2*. I planned out the evening, and it transpired exactly as I planned.

We enjoyed the movie together, laughing at scenes we thought were ridiculous, her cringing at scenes that were more graphic. As the credits started to roll, she reached out to hold my hand and found a box sitting in my palm. I watched her eyes, watched her neurons firing, trying process what was happening. Tears filled her eyes as I finally spoke. "Will you marry me?"

She nodded, unable to speak, and we embraced. The rest of the night, she was walking on clouds. She didn't stop touching me once. I was happy as well. I had been exposed to some of the worst people possible throughout my life. The majority of them filled me with anger and hatred. She, on the other hand, made that anger disappear. I always tried to control my impulses by isolating myself, but after I stormed out of the classroom, I realized that isolation was a temporary bandage. I truly believed this woman was the key to help me with my control.

We were married within a few months. We decided on something small since I didn't have the lengthiest guest list. When we compared the lists, mine included my teacher at my dojo and a couple of people from work, which I'd only included because having no list seemed weird. Her list was close to fifty people: friends, family, and people from her past.

I was fine with the different numbers because I was already very aware of the differences in how many people we cared about. I only cared that she was present. However, the list sparked enough curiosity in her that she finally started to ask more about my family. Apparently, not speaking to my family was perfectly acceptable. Not inviting them to my wedding was odd enough that it warranted questioning. I tried to avoid the conversations as best as possible at first, or offered vague platitudes to quench her curiosity, but none of that worked. She knew I was dodging. I finally caved and told her more about them. I told her that my father was often absent, physically or mentally. I told her how my mother did nothing but try to put me down. I told her that sibling rivalry in my house meant sabotage or manipulation, and there were very few nice moments.

After I shared a few specific stories, she was shocked. She instantly developed a strong hatred toward my mother for the things she would say, and for my father, who did little to stop it. She apologized for ever asking and suggested we have a courthouse wedding so that the ceremony wouldn't be so heavily one-sided. Another display of understanding and compassion that still confuses me.

Married life didn't seem all that different honestly. We did the same things, we spoke the same way; we saw each other the same amount of time. We decided to stay in my apartment after the wedding until I finished school and my residency. It was easier to save money this way so we could eventually get the house we really desired. She didn't mind and stated that she felt like it was just as much her home as it was mine.

A couple of months after the wedding, the inevitable happened. She became pregnant. When she first gave me the news, I was terrified. Children added a level of stress to life for which I couldn't properly prepare. They were wildcards. But I did the correct thing and played like I was excited.

A few months into the pregnancy, she started to experience health concerns that resulted in her being on bed rest. I wasn't angry at her for the health she couldn't control. However, I was frustrated, because we were unable to have sex until the concerns had passed. I'd stopped having sex with other women shortly after she moved in with me. I was getting more than enough relief at home, and my schedule didn't permit it. After only a couple of weeks into her bedrest and without sex, though, I noticed my aggressive tendencies were becoming amplified. I was irritable, and my wife and I were bickering more. I knew the solution.

I didn't have time to go out weekly and find a new sexual partner. Luckily, I had taken my now-wife's advice and taken that job at the hospital. It was there that I met a woman. She was a nurse with short-cut blond hair and a figure that appeared nice in her scrubs. She always talked about her busy schedule and how she didn't have time for a full-fledged relationship. She would also flirt with me and make comments about having a more "friend with benefits" type of arrangement.

I took her up on her offer. The relationship progressed quickly, seeing as the only factor that needed considering was when and where to have sex. We skirted any emotional topics, and all of our post-coitus conversations centered around work. Since we worked together, it was easy to make time, and we were soon having sex two or three times a week. The balancing act of school, work, pregnant wife, martial arts, and sexual partner was quite a handful. Still, I managed well enough for about two months.

One day while at home, lying in bed with my wife, I received a text. I looked at my phone and saw it was from the nurse. I kissed my wife on the forehead and excused myself to the other room, where I read the text: *I need to speak with you now. Emergency!*

I'm not a foolish man. Our relationship wasn't deep. Whatever this emergency was, it had to be confined to the risks that were present in our dynamic. I knew it could only be that other staff members at the hospital had discovered our relationship, or she was pregnant. My heart began to race. This was not a stressor that I needed to deal with.

I gathered myself and told my wife that I needed to go to work. There was an issue at the hospital, and they were asking for anyone who could help to come. She was understanding, as she always was. I got dressed in work attire and gave her a kiss before leaving. I asked her if she wanted anything when I came back, and she requested cantaloupe (her current pregnancy craving).

I called the nurse from the car and asked where to meet her. She said a coffee shop about thirty minutes from my house, so I sped off in that direction.

I am usually composed until faced directly with a threat, but not in that moment. My mind was racing. I hoped my biggest concern was that someone had discovered us. It would be easy enough to explain away accusations if I was fired. I would just tell my wife that someone started a rumor, and it grew out of control. A pregnancy would be much more complicated. At this point, I was having a hard time feeling connected with the fetus that was gestating inside of my wife. I had a hard time connecting with anyone, much less an unborn someone that I had never met. However, I was trying to connect with the idea of being a father, because I cared for my wife.

A zygote in the womb of a woman that I could only stand long enough to achieve climax was completely different. My panic boiled over, and a hint of anger simmered under the surface.

How could this woman have let herself get pregnant? And why call me? Just get rid of it. This was not my problem to deal with. I had money set aside for emergencies, so I would offer to pay for the abortion if my assumption was accurate. In a month's time, this would no longer even register as important enough to remember. At least, that was what I told myself to help regain a sense of calm.

I pulled up to the coffee shop and saw the nurse

sitting at a table outside. Beads of sweat on her forehead, a blank stare, and her unkempt appearance all conveyed the level of panic she was in. I climbed out of my car and walked up to take a seat across from her. A moment of relief appeared on her face.

"Thank god you came. I didn't know if you would." Her voice showed signs of her crying recently.

"Of course. You said it was an emergency. I assumed you meant that." I kept my voice even and low. I wanted to study her while giving no hints as to my current state. "What's going on?"

Then she said the two words that confirmed my fears: "I'm pregnant." I took a long, deep breath. I mentally started beating myself up. I had been so careful in the beginning. I wore a condom, she was on the pill, and I still would pull out. However, more recently, I had been taking more risks. I forgot the condom on occasion, and didn't feel like pulling out. I couldn't believe that I was careless enough to trust the pill she *claimed* to take and not exert my own control over the situation. I chalked it up the stresses of my wife being on bedrest, but I knew that was a piss poor excuse at best.

She was looking at me, waiting for some form of response. I refused to supply it. I wasn't certain of how to have this conversation, so I decided to let her lead. If I could find my opening, I could ensure she got the abortion and be done with this situation. "I'm sorry to spring this on you. My period has been late, and I was feeling kind of nauseous. I took a test this morning, and it was positive." I remained silent while she stared at me. Finally, she broke the silence. "Can you say something?"

How had I not guessed that she would say that? The propensity in some people to need input before stating their desires is aggravating. I looked at her calmly and said, "Okay. Well, this is fairly simple to take care of. And I will pay for the whole thing. No need to be worried."

Her face was horrified. "What do you mean, take care of? I'm going to keep it."

I felt my face contort into confusion. I expected her to not know how she wanted to proceed, but not to be so resolute in her decision to keep it. We had no real meaningful relationship, so she would be raising this thing on her own. I didn't understand her motivation. "Why would you keep it? That's going to be a lot of work on you."

"Look, hear me out. I've been feeling a lot more connected to you the last couple of weeks, and I can tell you have been to."

"You can tell?" I interrupted. My voice was heavy with a mocking doubt.

"Yeah. We've been getting together more often. You've been choosing to see me instead of going home to your wife. The sex is so passionate. You can't deny it. And maybe this baby is a sign that we should be together."

She sounded so sincere, as if she really believed the words falling off her tongue. I knew the truth. Her brain was filled with dopamine and oxytocin from the increased attention and sex. She wasn't wrong that I had spent more time with her the last couple of weeks—it was because my wife was needing more sleep during her recovery. The sex was passionate because I preferred to keep the act more carnal and feral, rather than intimate and emotional. Her ovulation caused her to develop more intense feelings for me in hopes of this outcome. It was all easily explained through chemical reactions in her brain. However, she essentially knew nothing about me. She didn't understand that the idea that I loved her in some form was much closer to science-fiction than romance.

I didn't respond. There is no correct response to someone that's delusional. If you argue, they might become angry and spiteful. If you agree, you further entrench their delusion. We stayed in silence for several minutes before she reached her hand out and placed it palm up on the table, hoping I would take the invitation and grasp it.

"I know this wasn't planned and that it's a lot. I'm not going to stop you from supporting your wife while she's pregnant or seeing your other child. I just think you would be happier with me."

The panic that had previously inhabited my body was gone. I narrowed my eyes and looked from her outstretched hand to her face. "I need to think about this. Give me some time and space to process all of this." I stood up calmly to leave the table.

Her face was filled with sadness and disappointment, but she designed her words to be reassuring. "Of course. Take all the time you need."

I walked back to my car, climbed in, and started driving. This woman had apparently lost her mind. Maybe I failed to see some sort of instability there to begin with, but this was too far. Her and that thing growing in her threatened my marriage, threatened to destroy the happiness of my wife, and were a hindrance on the potential relationship with the unborn fetus I had accepted as mine. Her grasp exceeded her reach, and I would not allow her to bring my life to ruins. I felt a familiar chill distribute itself through my system.

I had my plan made by the time I parked my car. I walked into my home and woke my wife with a kiss and a container filled with cantaloupe. This was where I wanted to be and where I belonged. No one, alive now or as of yet unborn, would take it.

Nine days. That was how long I waited. If I had acted too soon, it would've been obvious to anyone that knew of our conversation that it was me. Nine days. A bit on the long side for processing big news, but still reasonable with the weight of my current situation. Just long enough that people could assume I might be avoiding, or I might be struggling, but certainly not plotting. Perfect timing in my mind.

I knew the nurse's schedule because it was easily available to me at the hospital. I knew where she lived because of our sexual encounters. I knew her patterns because our life had been intertwined for several months and she liked to chat. My wife was on bed rest and sleeping like a coma patient, so she wouldn't notice my coming or going. Everything was perfect.

I went to bed that Wednesday night with my wife but did not allow myself the comfort of sleep. I rose at about 3 a.m. I got dressed in a pair of old black jeans that I kept for lawn work, a long-sleeve black shirt, and a pair of old hiking shoes that had outlived their usefulness. All clothing that no one would question my getting rid of. I made sure that every piece of clothing was perfectly clean the day before while my wife rested. Not a single hair or food crumb to be found. I stole a pair of latex gloves from work that I put in my pocket. I had an old hockey mask from the year prior when my wife insisted we dress up to hand out candy on Halloween.

I drove to the nurse's neighborhood and parked several blocks down. I walked the distance and arrived in her yard a little after four. I knew she left for her twelve-hour shift on Thursdays at about five. I chose a comfortable place in the shadows of the corner of her house, where I could clearly see her driveway. Her compact SUV was parked where it always was so that she could stumble out, half-asleep, and reach out on muscle memory alone. I kneeled, put the mask on, and waited.

During my wait, the early-morning air was crisp and sharp on my skin, but I paid it no mind. I was here with a goal and nothing else penetrated my thoughts but that goal. The neighborhood was quiet. The dark morning brought with it a sense of peace to everywhere it extended except for the two square feet I occupied. I heard her front door creak open, and a yawn followed by a tiny squeak as she exited her home. I watched as she mindlessly made her way to her car, like a zombie following some instinct for its destination.

As she got closer to her car, I began to move. I stayed upright and silent, the latex gloves now hugging the flesh of my hands. When she got close enough to her car to reach for the handle, I pounced. My hand found the back of her head and slammed it forward. Her skull made a loud thud as it bounced off of the driver's-side window. Then a second. Then a third. On the third collision of her face and glass, I held her head in place. I didn't apply enough pressure to cause extreme pain, just enough to ensure that if she still had the energy to fight back, she couldn't. I then delivered three powerful uppercuts to her right kidney. She didn't scream or yelp. I wasn't certain if she was conscious, but I was fairly sure she had a concussion.

I released her head, and she fell to the ground. The window that she'd been pinned to was smeared with blood. I looked down at her face, and it looked like something close to raw steak, a red mess. Her mouth hung open, and I could see at least one of her front teeth missing. I wasn't done, though. I'd come with a mission, and it was time to complete it.

I used my foot to turn her body onto the side, and she offered no resistance. I began sending my foot into her abdomen over and over. After the first kick, she made her first sound. Through her bloodied and damaged face, she muttered two simple words: "Please...no."

Her chance to stop this had ended the moment she suggested I leave my wife.

I wasn't sure how many times I kicked her, but by the end I was certain that what I came to accomplish was indeed accomplished. I looked down at the pitiful mess lying under my feet and felt only a small growing sense of success.

This person had thought she knew better than me. She thought that she could tell me what I wanted and needed. Her ego had swelled to such extents that she deluded herself into believing she could ever share a life with me, much less understand me. She was the effigy of all the people that had told me how I should be living my life and what was best for me. Images of my mother telling me to stop trying because I wouldn't amount to anything and that I should be happy with what I was given flashed through my mind. The words of numerous girls that believed they could "heal me with their love" rang in my ears. I leaned down, grabbed her purse, and pulled her wallet from it. Then I dropped the bag and left.

I did not want her dead. The problem existed within her uterus. Without that obstacle, she was nothing but a petty and needy victim that would seek solace from a coworker. Everything was set up to look like a random attack or robbery.

I went to a spot that I would sometimes frequent when I needed to get away from people. It was a wooded area that would get very busy around the summertime and on weekends for those that enjoyed hiking or camping. I knew it should be fairly empty that Thursday.

I found a camping spot with a fire pit and gathered wood to start a fire. I kept an extra set of work clothes in the car in case I ever needed them. I stripped down and changed in the car as the fire grew bigger. Then I sat on a log by the fire and used a knife I kept on my person to begin shredding the clothing I'd worn. The blade was about seven inches long and I kept it very sharp, so it made quick work of the fabric. The shoes were a bit more difficult, but I was still able to remove most of the material from the sole and cut it into strips. Over the next hour, I burned all of the clothes, the gloves, and the contents of her wallet. I didn't necessarily need to burn the money, but I didn't want anything of hers on me. It wasn't fear of being caught, it was the disgust of having anything that reminded me of her.

I returned home and found my wife still sleeping soundly in our bed. I looked at her with a sense of comfort, knowing that our marriage was no longer at risk. I kissed her sleeping head and went into work.

Halfway through my shift, the news of the nurse started to spread. She was actually admitted to the same hospital that we worked at. I went to visit her room and see how she was doing. She had a concussion, a fractured orbital socket, a broken jaw, a lacerated kidney, four broken ribs—and she'd suffered a miscarriage. She was not conscious, but I didn't need to speak with her. Once her attending told me about the miscarriage, I had all the information I needed.

In the following weeks, she reached out to me several times to come over and support her. I was conveniently busy for the first couple weeks, and then I stopped responding completely. Her physical therapy took several months, and by the time she returned to work, I had left to start my residency at a different hospital. My actual seed was born several months later, and I never gave her another thought.

10

HAPPINESS

People talk about the things that make them happy all the time, but do they really understand what they are saying? Are they truly happy or just feeling a moment of relief from the suffering concurrent with mere existence?

Happiness is a simple emotion to understand at its core. Yet most people mistake merely being content as the same thing. I am jealous of people who are actually able to feel happy. I have felt things akin to happiness, but I have never experienced overwhelming joy. I did feel gracious when my wife accepted my proposal, because she'd accepted such a vulnerable request. I didn't feel happy, though. And with the nurse, I felt not happiness but relief.

I don't know how often I have actually felt happy, or if I ever have. There's never been a challenge I wasn't positive that I could overcome. With sufficient effort and manipulation, anything is achievable, so what is there to celebrate? My life has been heavily burdened with struggle, but each struggle was either self-imposed or a facet of life that I was unable to control. Either way, I could easily overcome it with the exertion of enough effort. My mother hated me, so I moved out. I was raised in an environment that didn't support my academic achievement, so I studied. It was fairly simple.

It's odd that people put joy on a pedestal when compared to the rest of the emotional spectrum. People will go to great lengths to avoid sadness, fear, anger, or stress, because these are negative emotions in their perspective. Happiness is the only good one. Regardless of what they are feeling, they convince themselves it is happiness, because that means they are doing good.

Even if it were possible to be genuinely happy at all times, I would find that incredibly boring. Happiness is only enjoyable because it provides a reprieve from misery. If you were to eat your favorite food for three meals a day, every single day, how long before the mere scent of it would repulse you? It's the cheap sandwiches, slightly burnt pizzas, and undercooked pasta that accentuate the favorite dish. If any person could feel happy solely because they wished for it, the experience would be insignificant.

People cannot experience happiness if they don't experience pain. I appreciate my wife to the extent that I do because first I experienced the hatred of my family. I wouldn't understand how meaningful support would be if I didn't know how dangerous a lack of support was. If I could turn back time, I wouldn't change a thing. All of my suffering resulted in me finding something that I value.

There are two reasons that most people are unhappy and will stay that way indefinitely. First, they are not honest and genuine with themselves. I know who I am. I know what makes me happy. Martial arts make me happy because I have a natural inclination toward violence. I have worked with patients who can identify the activities or accomplishments that would bring them some form of joy, but they deny themselves the sensation because other people view it as weird or wrong. It shouldn't matter if people think it's odd to go back to college at forty or build a blanket fort in your house. If something speaks to who you are and can make you happy, then do it.

Second, we do not cherish stress and pain the way we should. Pain and discomfort are indicators of growth. Training, learning, and working causes discomfort. These are not sensations that should be avoided; they should instead be honored. What pride comes from an achievement that was obtained with ease? The pain is what makes it a worthwhile endeavor. People try so hard to avoid discomfort. Yet pain inspires true pride and confidence within us.

In my work I often encounter people who have all the keys to happiness, yet are scared to unlock the door because of the fear of struggle. I encourage them to challenge themselves and jump feet first into dark waters. If you are unhappy in your marriage, confront your partner. Will it be difficult and, most likely, uncomfortable? Almost certainly. However, how can the relationship change without that confrontation? Whether you choose to confront them or leave them, at least you make progress up the slope that leads to a land of joy. Staying still and making no decisions or meaningful changes is the easy option, because there's no unknown and there's no failure.

Embrace discomfort. Embrace fear. Embrace stress. Embrace pain. These are the only true indicators of our effort in this world.

11

With the birth of my first child, life did not become any easier. I enjoyed living with my wife previously because she afforded me the freedom to participate in all of the same activities I always had. She was never controlling by any stretch. I was still active in my dojo and was able to work without incessant texts about inane topics like how much she missed me. She would still text statements like that, but never with the expectation of a response. It was a good life.

After finishing med school and leaving the hospital, I started my residency. Luckily, the university that I went to for med school accepted me into their residency program. It was around that time that my wife gave birth, and everything started to shift for me. My professional schedule became hectic. It seems the less you are paid, the more a supervisor wants you to work. The work itself wasn't particularly stressful, and dealing with patients was always fairly easy for me. My peers continued to struggle more in this area because of their high levels of compassion and their foolish self-imposed obligation to "help." I didn't struggle with this issue, so for me it was mostly just the schedule that caused difficulty.

An added layer of stress was that the expectation to be present in my household increased dramatically. This was completely new to me. I was barely a partici-pating member in my own immediate family as a child, and now I was expected to be a father and a hus-band on a daily, and sometimes hourly, basis. I would come home and prepare a ritual to ensure my contin-ued level of self-control, but my wife would want to talk about her day. Every single day. And to be hon-est, her day was never that interesting. She decided to quit her job permanently after having the baby so she could stay home and be a mother full-time. That meant every day she was home with a baby and doing chores. There are only so many experiences that she could have in that environment, and I heard them all multiple times.

We were still living in the little two-bedroom apart-ment that had previously been just mine. We main-tained our plan of wanting to keep the apartment until I finished my residency and started work in earnest so we could afford something nice. The apartment was great when I first moved in and was single. It was still good when it was just my wife and me. However, it was not great for a family with an infant child. The walls seemed paper thin at times, so we had to be careful about our volume when the baby was sleeping. The worse part was I didn't really have an escape. My second bedroom had previously been dedicated to providing me a space to study, but it also gave me a place to get a break from my wife when my social battery had been depleted. Now, that was the baby's room, and I was always around my wife.

Still, I catered to her desire, recognizing that venting about the monotony of her life was necessary to maintain her sanity. It is a testament to how much I care for her that I never looked her in the face and told her to shut her mouth. Any other human would have been lucky with even that disrespectful response.

Then there was the child. It was born a girl, and cute by every standard that we hold child appearance. My first was nothing truly remarkable as a baby. I expected to feel some sudden shift in myself the first time I held her, but it didn't occur. I was struggling to connect with an individual that did nothing but eat, sleep, and defecate. Everyone said that she was so smart and so funny. How exactly is a baby either of those things? She is unaware of her own surroundings, yet she is smart because she allows herself to be guided by base curiosity and impulse. If I did that, it would be completely dangerous and extremely socially unacceptable. She's funny because she lacks complete muscle control and her head rolls around sometimes? People talk about babies in the oddest ways.

Everyone in my wife's life liked to make comments about how being the father of a daughter would change me somehow. That I would become more protective and more anxious. I never noticed it. They said they were excited to see me when she went on her first date someday, because I would be cleaning my gun as the would-be suitor came to pick her up. That entire concept was ridiculous. As if I would ever make such a public spectacle out of my desire or plan to harm someone. The truth is, I cared for her because she was my first child with my wife, and therefore she was my responsibility.

The toll the increased stress had on me was substantial. I stopped sleeping with other girls. It was partially due to the incident with the nurse and not wanting a repeat of that, but also because I didn't have time. The first year or so after my daughter was born, my wife and I barely had sex. Without martial arts and without sex, my level of irritability and aggression slowly started to creep up. I would intentionally look for ways to start conflict at home. I'm by no means stupid, but I would purposefully tell my wife when the baby was crying and then do nothing to help. I knew I was fully capable of holding her or feeding her, but I needed an outlet for my pent-up energy, and our arguments became that for me.

Our fights never became physical, but they were definitely hostile. After my first was a year old, the arguments had escalated to screaming and comments designed to cause deep emotional damage. I'm not the only guilty party; she certainly took part in this behavior as well. But I knowingly pushed her into it. I would start an argument about something miniscule, like her not texting from the grocery store to see if I wanted anything. I would throw fuel on the fire by being aggressive and disrespectful. She would inevitably become defensive, and I would immediately be calm and gaslight her into thinking she was the aggressor.

It was a significant improvement on how I might have expressed my inner desires to another person.

The stressful environment was not helped by our neighbors. They were another young married couple that loved to argue. I saw the immediate similarities, but what made them so much more annoying was both of their desires to vent to my wife and me about their problems. It sometimes seemed like the husband would listen for when I stepped outside to have a cigarette, and he would ambush me with complaints about his wife. I would be trying to relax and correct myself, then all of a sudden, he was there.

"Can you believe women these days?" he would say to me. The truth was, I never understood what he meant by that. Conflict takes two people, so he was equally responsible for their fights. I would nod and not respond verbally, hoping that would be enough of a hint that my true desire was solitude. It never worked.

"I work all day, and as soon as I step through the door, she's on my ass. She's always bitching about the laundry and the dishes and the floors. You don't hear me bitching about my day at work."

That was a lie. I could clearly hear him complain about his day a lot of the time. I would continue to nod though, knowing that challenging his statement would only lengthen my exposure to him.

"Sometimes I just want to strangle her so she'll shut up." This was a sensation I was very familiar with, seeing as I felt that way toward him during each of these interactions.

He would go on like that until I finished my cigarette, then wish me luck in dealing with my wife. I didn't need the luck; I was the instigator and aware of it. Plus, I never felt the desire to harm her. He seemed like he was in much greater need of that than me.

The neighbor wife, meanwhile, would unload onto my wife. Sometimes I'd come home to them sitting at the dining room table as she described, in far too great of detail, an argument from the previous night. Simultaneously, she would paint her husband as a horrible and violent narcissist. I don't think her diagnosis was accurate, but she never struck me as very learned. He struck me as moderately to severely depressed, which he displayed as anger, coupled with an ever-building resentment toward her. I would excuse myself quickly anytime I found these conversations occurring.

My wife told me that she never complained about me during their discussions, and that their talks made her appreciate me more. She would complain about the conversations to me, and on several occasions vocalized concern for the woman's well-being. I like to think I had gotten much better at feigning empathy when she would talk to me about her day, but it was almost impossible for me to even care enough to try and fake concern for two people that I genuinely disliked.

And so life went for about a year. Work, wife, daughter, annoying neighbors, and repeat. Our arguments continued to escalate throughout the months, and at the one-year mark after our first was born, we had a conversation. She acknowledged that I had a lot going on and she was feeling lonely. Then she admitted she was putting her loneliness on me to fix. She decided that it would be most helpful if she and our child went to visit her parents for a few weeks. She thought this would give me the time alone I needed to reset, and her the social time she needed to feel human again. I immediately agreed.

She had continued to maintain a strong relationship with her parents, but their visits had dwindled since we had a child. I thought they were nice enough, though I never rejoiced at the prospect of listening to her father talk about sports or politics whenever we visited. This solution killed multiple birds with one stone. She would get to see her family, which would help her. I would have a good reason to avoid interacting with her family. And we would both get a break from each other. I did enjoy her presence in my life, and I was rather fond of my daughter. However, they were always around, and the constancy of their presence was beginning to become more than slightly irritating.

I never wanted to hurt either of them. I didn't once experience a true desire to cause them harm. For lack of any better term, I loved them. But that love didn't make it easy to listen to the day-to-day complaints or change diapers one after the other. How does a single tiny human create so much urine and feces? On several occasions, I would change her diaper, only for her to immediately soil the next one the moment it was sealed.

Regardless, they left town. I kissed them both

goodbye and agreed to get any necessary tasks completed around the house. I went inside and immediately began watching some of the extremely graphic horror movies that I had begun finding for some minor relief. Films like *August Underground, Cannibal Holocaust, 120 Days of Sodom*, and *A Serbian Film*. I never recommended these movies to the average person that might ask, and I refused to watch them with anyone. Based on reviews I had read, the average viewer would become upset, angry, or nauseated at viewing these films, and I didn't want anyone to see that I truly enjoyed them. I recognized that I was vicariously living through the antagonists of these films and their ability to inflict violence with minimal repercussions, and I didn't want that enjoyment to be visible to others.

Several days passed, and I went about my normal schedule with the exception of taking care of other people. I was enjoying the peace of solitude when it was suddenly interrupted by the escalation of voices in conflict. The neighbors were arguing again, and their hostility was creeping into the cracks of my pleasure and eroding it to a lump of irritation. I paused the film I was watching, *I Spit on Your Grave*, and attempted to do some breathing and meditation exercises to bring myself back down. It was not successful. This argument seemed more heated than normal. I finally decided to take action when I heard a loud thud and the breaking of glass.

I went to see what had happened. If nothing else, I would get them to shut up so I could enjoy my movie. The thought of walking into an already aggressive situation empty handed made me feel naked and vulnerable, so I grabbed the seven-inch knife that I still kept on my person most of the time and walked out the front door.

The moment I was standing in the fresh air of nature, the intensity of their argument became amplified, free now from the dulling effects of our walls. As I locked my door, I saw the neighbor husband storm out of his apartment, slamming the door with a loud crash. I normally wouldn't have cared enough to go "check in" with either of them, but I had already put on pants and shoes, so I figured it would be most efficient if I walked over there anyway.

I approached the door and knocked out of politeness (and a small hope that she wouldn't respond and I could go home while saying I'd done what I could when my wife returned home). As soon as I knocked, the door flew open, and the neighbor wife stood there fuming like she was ready to attack. Once she realized it was me, her demeanor softened some, but it was easy to identify she was still in a frantic state.

"Hey," I said, "I heard some things breaking and just wanted to make sure that no one was hurt." This wasn't a complete lie. I did want to make sure that no one was hurt, because the sound of sirens for the remainder of the evening would truly interrupt my peace. She looked down and saw the knife in my hand and her eyes widened a bit. I immediately explained, "No, this was just in case there was a break-in or something. Sorry, I didn't mean to scare you."

Her demeanor softened even more as she responded.

"You're fine. It scared me a bit, but I'm sure after all that, you didn't want to come over empty-handed. Come in."

I took a bit of offense at her saying that I needed a weapon to defend myself, but I immediately dismissed it because, in my mind, she was an idiot. Her apartment was a wreck. There was what looked like the wreckage of a stack of plates that had been knocked off the counter. Glass littered the floor, and there were some overturned end tables. Her face was red, and a part of it was beginning to swell. The swelling wasn't localized enough to come from a fist, and I surmised that it mostly likely came from an open-hand slap.

As I surveyed the area, she began to ramble on about her night. "Can you believe that piece of shit? I ask him to help a little around the house, but he does absolutely nothing. He thinks because he has a job that he doesn't have to do anything around here. You have a job and you still help your wife." She began to pick things up as she spoke. With her last statement, she shut the door behind me. I stood awkwardly in the wreckage of an apartment I really didn't want to be in. Now, I felt trapped. I also didn't appreciate her comparing her husband to me. It was uncomfortable. She didn't know what I did or didn't do, and she didn't understand my motives behind anything. On top of that, I didn't like the mere idea of being compared to him. It was as if I were being compared to a piece of cattle or a mange-stricken dog. Insulting.

"Yeah, I guess so. I don't really know about your marriage. Plus, my wife needs help because of the baby."

I figured taking a more passive stance would allow me to slide out of this situation relatively unnoticed.

She continued to prattle on. "Yeah, we don't have a baby, because Mr. Works-All-The-Time can't get it up long enough to put one in me." All I could think was that I had done some bad things, but these people would be much worse parents than me. "Then, he wants to call me a crazy bitch because I break a few plates. I'm the one who cleans them, so I should get to do what I want with them."

The tension and aggressive energy of the conversation was starting to eat at me. It felt like a small worm of anger burrowing into my ear to eventually rest and spread through my brain. I understood what she was saying, but I also understood that it was a completely ridiculous situation. She was mad about washing dishes, which was foolish because everyone had to do it at some point. Breaking them all only created a bigger mess and more responsibility to buy more. This was getting stupid. I finally spoke up: "I mean I wouldn't say it was crazy, but it was a bit destructive."

This was apparently the wrong thing to say, and I'd thought I was being tactful. Her head whipped at me, and the anger that was in her eyes when she first opened the door returned. "Destructive? No, it is destructive for him to say that he is going to get a hotel room for the night because he can't deal with me. That destroys marriages, and it's a lot easier to buy plates than build a marriage. What do you know? Your wife had to leave town to get away from you."

Now, the insult wasn't just perceived—that was a

direct attack. My blood didn't boil, though. Her insults felt like the yapping of a small puppy that thought it could protect itself.

Any faux compassion I was attempting to portray was replaced with an icy stare and apathy. "My wife left town because she is busy all day and needed a break. She doesn't work, so she takes care of our child and our home. I help because I see the effort she puts toward our relationship and want to help. Maybe if you did the same, your husband would be here right now for you to verbally assault instead of me."

I knew the comment would sting, but I was tired of restraint. My movie had been interrupted by two grown individuals that couldn't handle cohabitating but refused to leave. She wanted to use me as a verbal punching bag since her normal target was MIA. I got so little time to myself that I wanted her to know what a pain in the ass she was.

Apparently, she didn't get the message. She stood up straight and took several long strides to reach me. She dug her finger into my chest and began berating me with every insult her below-average intellect could muster. "Oh, you make an effort? Your wife told me all about how you used to whore around town. I bet you still do. Probably to make up for that tiny package in your pants. You're probably no better than my husband."

Her words meant nothing to me. I had no problems with my anatomy, had heard no complaints, and wouldn't have cared if I had. Fighting your anatomy is like being mad that the sky is blue.

The thing that bothered me was that finger stabbing

me in the chest. She was applying pressure, I assumed to push me back, but I refused to move.

"You think you're a big man coming over here to rescue the damsel in distress. You're just like my husband, think that everyone around you needs to bow down and kiss your feet. You probably think everyone wants to be like you and every girl wants a piece of your pathetic ass. Too bad for you I wouldn't fuck a freak like you if you pai—"

Her voice stopped. I felt warmth start to spread down my hand and then my arm. I hadn't taken my eyes off of hers the entire time she was this close, and I still didn't. I watched her rage-filled glare suddenly shift into shock and confusion. I watched as she looked down and to her left, and my eyes followed hers. I'm sure my face looked confused as well at this moment. Not a shock or fearful confusion, but a confusion of analysis. I saw my hand, clutching my knife. It was covered in thick red fluid. My eyes traced from my arm to my hand to the blade to the entry point in the side of her neck. That was the source of the fluid.

My gaze returned to her eyes. Her lips parted, and blood began to trickle from between them, accompanied by the guttural sounds of her gurgling on her own blood. Her eyes pleaded with me to remove the blade and call for help, but I didn't move. I was glued to the spot with the same interest and anticipation of a child on Christmas Day. I held the knife firmly and watched as her eyes went from panicked and pleading to completely lifeless. I caught her body as it started to fall with my other hand and lowered her to the ground so it wouldn't make any loud noise. I removed the knife from her throat, and it slid out with extreme ease. People in movies compare it to pushing a knife through butter, but this felt different. It was more solid, but the knife found no resistance at all.

I stood up and replayed the events. Her anger and aggression had gotten me worked up early on. Her personal attacks had indicated that she was an enemy. Her physical contact with me made it clear she had no intention of backing down. None of that was the actual reason my arm moved on reflex to quiet the cow, though. It was her inane talking. She was blaming her husband for her behavior. Then she blamed me when she was challenged. She was a complete imbecile that required there to be another person responsible for her actions.

It's almost impossible to completely describe the feelings I had at that moment. I was not excited, angry, or happy. I guess I could best describe it as relief. I felt like an air mattress that was letting out its air. Tension that I had been unknowingly holding in my body for decades slowly started to release itself. I had been dealing with stupid and judgmental people since the day I was born, and, my best guess was I had been holding in my desire to end their tyrannical reign of thickheadedness for decades. I stood there and stared at her body. There was no sympathy or guilt in that moment. There was a small amount of pride in finally getting her to shut her mouth. I had rid the world of a truly toxic and unchanging creature. I was no hero. I didn't deserve adulation or a parade. But I did feel like I deserved to pat myself on the back for doing something that so many before me should have done.

There was one other sensation that swept across my being. A feeling I had never experienced before. For as long as I could remember, I had attempted to restrain myself as best I could to follow the social etiquette I'd been force-fed my whole life. I did what I *should* have done. I acted the way I was *supposed to* act. I allowed the world around me to shackle my hands and feet, then place me in a cell of conservative societal morality. In that moment, though, I felt freedom. I had, for the briefest period, cast off the manacles. I did not worry if I should've been more controlled or more restrained. I didn't think about anything I should have done. Feeling the weightlessness that accompanied my lack of regard for the "right thing to do" almost felt like flying.

I quickly devised a plan and went to work. Several hours later, I found myself back on my couch, enjoying the remainder of the movie that had been so rudely interrupted earlier.

The next day I was woken by a knock at the door. I knew who it was and casually went to greet them. I couldn't move too quickly, because that could cause suspicion. My lungs burned slightly from the fire in the woods the night prior, where I'd burned my clothes. My hair was still damp from the thorough showering I gave myself. My sense of smell still lingered with the smoke from my clothes and that river water that always seems to stick in your nasal passages, but it was necessary to dispose of the knife. I would miss that knife.

I opened the door wearing my pajama pants and a plain white T-shirt. On the other side was a uniformed police officer. There were several people moving around behind him. Some were other officers, and some looked like forensic types (based solely on my knowledge from law enforcement shows). The sun was just now starting to rise, casting an almost eerie pale light across the scene. I adopted a confused and concerned face. "Can I help you, Officer?"

Stalwart in his professionalism, he looked me in the eyes. "Sir, I'm sorry to wake you. I need to ask you a few questions about an incident last night. Did you hear any type of commotion from your neighbors over there?"

I looked down as if trying to replay the night's entire series of events in order to recollect my knowledge. "I mean, I heard a little bit of some fighting, but I'm really not trying to get anyone in trouble here. Did one of them call the cops?"

His appearance didn't shift. "Sir, it's important that you tell me everything as honestly as possible."

I took a deep breath. "Well, I don't remember what time it was because I was just watching a movie, but I did hear a lot of yelling—and some glass breaking."

"Why didn't you call 9-1-1, sir?"

"Honestly, it happens a lot with those two. We've seen police go to their door before, but nothing ever happens. I didn't think it was worth wasting more police hours for the officers to not be able to do anything." I thought it was important to be as dismissive as possible, while referencing actual facts that the officer would already know from looking up past calls.

"We?" My strategy must've worked if he thought that was the only piece that needed clarification.

"Yes, Officer. My wife and I have seen it. She's been out of town for several days though." I paused for a moment. "Can I ask what happened?" Normal people were always attracted to tragedy and never missed an opportunity to inquire about some.

"Sir, can you finish with last night's events?"

"Of course. After I heard some glass breaking, I heard the door open and slam shut. After that, there was some crying for a bit, then some silence. A little later, I heard the door open again and some muffled talking. I honestly assumed that they were making up from their fight and went to bed."

"Well, sir, I hate to inform you of this..." He told me she'd been killed last night, then paused, waiting for my reaction.

I knew enough about trauma and grief through my studies and interactions with patients that it was relatively easy to fake. You pause for a brief moment in complete disbelief. You stand there shocked as if waiting to hear it's a joke. Then you freeze as if you want to ask more, but take on a small amount of fear to stop yourself. Finally, you finish the process with, "What? No. That can't be. I just saw her yesterday."

The police officer then ran through what he knew. They'd received a call from the husband that he had found his wife dead. The police arrived at the scene and found the apartment completely demolished (as I had first seen it when I arrived, and how I left it when I left. I guess it was somewhat rude to ruin the last productive thing she had done before she died). The husband claimed to know nothing but had been taken in for questioning. As I listened to the officer speak, I began to intentionally look like I was holding back and heavily considering something. I couldn't just offer this piece of information. I needed him to smell the bait and bite.

"Sir, is there something you aren't telling me?" Mission accomplished.

"Please understand, I know I'm not a cop. So, I don't know if this is actually important. She comes over...came over a lot to speak with my wife. She has made comments about being worried about her safety at home. I never thought she meant in this type of way, though. If I had, I would've reported it immediately." I knew that if I didn't portray some guilt, shame, and regret, it would come off as insincere. The truth is, most people make tragedies about themselves. So, I followed suit.

The officer collected my name and asked if I would come to the station to make a formal statement. He asked for my wife's name and number, which I provided, but I first made sure he would let me tell her what happened. I wanted to support her emotionally when she first heard the news. That part was actually true.

I called my wife and told her what happened. She rushed home so she could give her statement to the police. She seemed more mad at herself for not seeing this coming. We both gave our statements.

The neighbor husband was eventually tried and found guilty of murdering his wife. Apparently, the long history of domestic disturbance complaints and witness statements from all of her friends about her previous comments about his temper was enough to destroy any perception of innocence in the jury's mind.

My wife and I agreed that we should move to a safer neighborhood. I still had a few years left of residency, but she expressed that she would rather move now and feel safe.

It seemed like after that incident, all of our arguments disappeared. She was convinced the husband had done it, and I guess she appreciated me more for how patient I was during our arguments. We decided to buy a house this time so that we wouldn't have to share a wall with any noisy neighbors. I requested a nice small place in a suburb that was within walking distance of some woods and a river.

12

JUSTICE

I despise the majority of people for many reasons, a significant one being that they refuse to be genuine and take accountability for themselves and their actions. I attempt to be as genuine as possible in my internal dialogue, while exerting great effort to hide who I am from others. A major motivator behind this incongruency is that I simply wanted to avoid justice. I don't mind admitting and recognizing my choices without pointing the finger at others, but the eventual karmic retribution for my actions looms over me heavily.

I don't think there is a true and objective idea of justice. Justice is based on two things, as far as I can tell: morality and reasoning. And if justice is about doing what is "right" and the idea of what is "right" is constantly changing, then what is justice? As a society we must have justice in order to avoid anarchy. A household must have justice if it hopes to operate. When a child steals from their parents, there should be a just punishment. If the punishment is too harsh, then the child will potentially feel like a victim and continue to resist the rule of the house. If the consequences are too lenient and not "fair" enough to the parents, then the child might not learn a lesson and will continue the behavior.

Reasoning is almost as difficult as morality. It is understandable logic to think that doing harm to another person is the wrong choice in almost every situation. However, I think that people that hinder the growth of society or cause undue stress on those around them should be wiped from the board. If a person does intentional harm to those they care about, and refuses to change, then there is no hope that they will ever be a fully functioning member of society. Dead weight does nothing but hold back progress.

Take the neighbor woman. She was violent, aggressive, and a drain on the person she was closest to. When confronted by others about her behavior, she was certain she had done no wrong. Worse yet, she desired to bring an innocent and impressionable infant into that environment. Would it have been logical to let her continue poisoning everyone with whom she built a relationship?

Her husband is still serving a life sentence for a murder he didn't commit. He was also far from innocent. He was already becoming violent with a woman that he refused to permanently sever ties with. He intentionally stayed in an environment that continued to breed anger, resentment, and violence, and showed no interest in changing any of this. Months I listened to him talk about how he wished he could strangle or beat his wife. What if he had left and his next partner had been more timid and he'd acted on it? I can't see the future, but I'm fairly confident that two people who genuinely thrive on chaos with no desire to improve will never become behaved.

At one point in time, there was the concept of "eye for an eye." On the surface, this makes perfect sense. Someone steals from you, you get his property. He kills your wife; you kill his wife. A completely reasonable approach. However, it falls short in the morality department. If the person that committed the first offense was wrong, then how is sinking to his level right? I wouldn't blame that husband for coming after me if he had ever discovered what I did, but that would make him just as much a monster as me.

The truth is justice is not about punishment or penance. It is an attempt to enforce the policies of the moral majority, and a method of keeping the rest in line. Hence why it is partially a moral obligation. It is subjective and vague. The idea of what is punishable changes over time.

I have never once thought that I needed to face the criminal justice system for the crimes that I have committed. I recognize they are crimes, as they go against the written laws of the country I live in. I just don't have strong feelings that I should be judged by tools of a system that is so easily influenced.

For the entirety of human history, people have

been sent to the gallows for their crimes. Death has been a part of criminal justice forever. Courts have made the judgment that a person is deserving of death based on a single moment in that person's life.

I make the same decision about other people's lives, but the evidence I gather is based on direct observations of someone's day-to-day decisions and interactions. I don't listen to expert testimony from a potentially biased professional being paid astronomical amounts of money to speak (and I have been that expert in court, so I know first-hand). I don't rely on the judgment of twelve random people bringing their own opinions and feelings to the equation. I have no emotional connection to my victims, no vested interest one way or the other. If I see evidence that they deserve life, I change my decision and move on.

It isn't the perfect form of justice, but does such a thing exist?

13

The following months were an interesting time for me. I had a lot of things I needed to process, obviously. I had always viewed my darker and more aggressive urges as something that should be restrained, confined, hidden as much as possible. I didn't know what would happen if I ever lost control. I always had imagined I would see red and lash out like a wild animal at everything near me.

I had technically lost control and acted purely from a place of impulse, but there was no wild animal lashing out. It was a pure and focused desire to eliminate the cause of my stress, which was standing in front of me.

I had to think back to all the situations before where I had lost control and become enraged. I didn't understand the differences at first. It took something my wife said during our move to help me understand. We were packing boxes into the car at one point, and I was attempting to be as efficient as possible by putting as much into the car at one time as I could. My wife looked at me and said, "Honey, be careful. The more you try to shove in there, the faster it'll come pouring out when we open the door." An extremely simple piece of logic that granted me a moment of enlightenment.

I had been trying to shove down my urges in all of those interactions to such an extent that when someone opened the door, rage poured out. I wasn't necessarily angry at them. I was angry at the feeling of holding myself back. Allowing myself to be convinced that I needed to fit into society in order to survive was my greatest stressor. I realized I didn't want to fit into society, or even appear as if I did. I hated "playing the game" with a girl in order to get what I wanted. I didn't see anything wrong with looking someone in the face and telling them that I planned to have sex with them and forget them the next day. I was exhausted and burnt out from putting on a fake smile day after day in order to increase others' comfort. If other people get uncomfortable with me, why is that my problem?

This realization might have come easier to me because I had my wife and first child by my side, accepting me. They didn't know anything, but they had never judged me to that point.

The moment I realized I had pushed that knife into the flesh of her neck, I felt unburdened. I felt like all of the boxes and bags had been freed from the confines of my body and I could breathe again. My wife is a truly insightful individual.

That wasn't the end of my thoughts, of course. My epiphany helped shed light on my life up to this point.

My level of awareness helped me know that I felt no change other than increased comfort. Now, I had to think about what that meant for my future. I couldn't go around killing every neighbor that pissed me off. I had no interest in prison, and I figured even the dumbest detective would connect the dots after a second body next door. I didn't want my family to be affected by my choices, so I knew I had to be careful.

The burning question that I didn't have an answer to was whether I wanted to do it again.

The release was comforting, but also a minimal payoff to the potential consequences. A fleeting moment of reprieve from the suffering of human existence is not substantial enough to risk life in prison. I knew that if my decision came solely from a desire to chase a dopamine release, I would eventually make a mistake like any other person that struggles with addiction. So that motivation was useless, and I immediately discarded it.

I didn't see a point in randomly killing strangers because it seemed "fun." I felt satisfaction in my first intentional kill because I truly felt that she deserved to die. She was a waste of human flesh. She had everything necessary to be a successful and happy person, but she squandered it. Her life would not improve, and I feel like I did a service by not allowing her to be the apple that rots the barrel. I would never get that satisfaction from killing someone on a whim.

I went in circles. My brain attempted to attack the question from multiple angles, but still I found no weak point to be exploited. Then I changed the question. If I was going to kill someone, who would it be?

The nurse didn't deserve to die. She may have been foolish, but her actions were most likely driven by shock and fear at the thing that was growing inside of her. My peers didn't strike me as meaningful targets; they were products of an overly compassionate society with a weak educational system. At least they were trying to do something with the weakness they had identified in themselves. My patients were completely off the table. They were all actually ill and attempting to improve. How could I stand in the way and punish someone for trying to be better?

Then it struck me, and still to this day I hate how cliche the answer is. If I could kill one person, it would be my mother.

It is humiliating to be reduced in my own mind to some poor boy with mommy issues. However, the idea made sense. She had been given every opportunity to change and had chosen not to. I watched as she belittled and berated my siblings and me, completely for her own self-affirmation that she was good and we were bad. She was no different than the neighbor wife.

These thoughts gave me even more to unpack. I did find it interesting that as I unpacked the belongings that represented me in the physical world into my new house, I was trying to unpack the thoughts that formed my identity in my newfound headspace. I was certain that I hadn't killed that woman because she reminded me of my mother. I know I'm not that pitiful, to only continue killing avatars for an actual desired target that was unattainable. No, I hated their personality. The self-assured, entitled, ignorant, and toxic behavior that would spread like wildfire and burn anyone that approached.

I also had to consider if I was so cliche that I only wanted to kill women. It seemed wrong, and more than a bit sexist. Men could have the exact same traits, and a lot of the time to a much greater degree. I had to have standards for myself, and targeting people based only on sex was unsatisfactory.

I knew I would never actually kill my mother. Not because of some genetic obligation to be caring though. I wouldn't do it because of two simple reasons. One, the police would obviously connect her to me. Second, since moving out, I hadn't spoken with her and now didn't know where to find her.

I went in circles and finally decided that I would not actively seek a target, but if one presented itself to me, I wouldn't hide from it. I felt this could be my purpose in life, but that was based on a single moment. Proper experimentation requires the results to be replicated in future experiments to verify reliability. If I killed some-one again, and didn't feel that I was fulfilling my pur-pose, then I would never do it again. If I never found someone that I thought was deserving, then my entire hypothesis was invalid and should be abandoned.

I went on with life as normal. A year passed after the incident with the neighbor. I became a licensed psychi-atrist. My marriage continued to improve. My daughter hit developmental milestones.

Everything was as it should be. I hadn't felt any urge to hurt anyone; my aggressive urges hadn't been sparked even once. No red-hot rage, no icy chill. I still was me, of course. I had no urge to make friends or even meet my wife's friends, but I did take a break from going to the dojo to better help with my daughter. I started to feel more connected to her and started to see her more as mine. I spent the bulk of my time at work or at home with my family. I even stopped experiencing any urge to sleep with other people. I was getting more than enough intimacy with my wife, so there was no true desire. It was a nice life that I truly thought I could live through for the rest of my days.

One day, I took my daughter to the store because we needed some groceries, and my wife was with her friends. I encouraged her to go out with her friends as much as she wanted. It helped her manage her level of irritability, but it also gave me the much-needed breaks from interacting. My daughter wasn't much of a handful; even in infancy, she was extremely independent. These shopping trips weren't bad, because she would eye all the pretty labels while I quickly got what we needed and left. Efficiency is the key to a calm life.

My daughter was particularly well-behaved that day, so I decided to be nice to her. I walked down the toy aisle and looked for some gadget that would help her increase whatever cognitive skills she was developing at the time. Plus, it would look nice to my wife and put points into my column the next time I irritated her. She sat in the cart while I walked up and down. I preferred to come to the stores in the middle of the day. My task could be completed more effectively if I wasn't encumbered by weaving in and out of the crowds.

As I turned the corner to continue my search for the toy aisle with items that were age appropriate, I witnessed a scene that still stays in my memory. It was a mother and father with their son and daughter. They had slightly tanned skin, but I couldn't tell if that was ethnicity or simply the current craze of basting oneself like a Thanksgiving turkey. The parents were both middle-aged, showing the typical signs of years of working and stress. The son was somewhere around six years old, based on height and how he was speaking, and the daughter must have been a couple of years older than him.

I watched as the boy picked up some type of doll in a pink box. It was the type that came with a couple of clothing accessories, and there were all types of extra convertibles and dream houses that were sold separately. He turned and looked up at his mother as he excitedly asked, "Mommy, can I have this one?" His question wasn't pleading or whiny, he did not act entitled, but his mother violently snatched it from his hands regardless.

She looked down with an irritated glare. "No, you cannot. This is a girl's toy, and you're a boy." I highly doubt the boy was confused about this concept unless his parents did very little to explain basic anatomy to the child. I was curious, because I couldn't comprehend what was wrong with him wanting the doll. Maybe he liked pink, or maybe one of his male dolls needed a wife. It seemed normal enough to me.

He looked confused. "Yeah, but look, she has extra shoes she can wear." His eyes stared into his mother's as if to nonverbally communicate his strong desire for the toy. Sure, it can be irritating when someone asks for something repeatedly, but the mother's problem seemed more related to gender than an overall irritation at constant questioning.

His father glanced behind him, as if to see if there was anyone close by. Then he returned his attention to the child. "Don't be so queer. Go get a toy for boys."

And with that, I understood. They were under the impression the boy would turn gay or something by playing with a doll. Ridiculous, but I knew I couldn't get mad at every irrational parent. They weren't aware that behaviors don't form personality. The behaviors we are drawn to are dictated by our personality. I didn't become what I am by playing with dead animals; I played with dead animals because I am what I am.

I was prepared to skip past the aisle to avoid any awkward moment where the parents tried to fake a smile as if I hadn't overheard them. As I prepared to step off, I glanced at the son one more time. His eyes filled with tears. I assumed primarily in response to being told no, but I had a strong suspicion that the father's unnecessary challenge of the boy's sexuality also played a role. I didn't feel sympathy for him, but I was more curious now about how the parents would respond to him.

I did not expect it. The mother's hand met the child's cheek with a loud smack. His face was beginning to turn red, and the tears started to pour but with no audible indicators escaping his mouth. "You do not need to cry over a doll. You are not going to be some fag playing with dolls. So stop your crying or I will stop it for you." Her gaze had turned from irritated to hateful.

I watched as the boy's older sister looked up at her father, pleading for him to stop what was happening. "Don't start that shit," he said. "Your brother is fine. He doesn't need to be crying like a little girl in the store. Get your crap and come on."

I watched as the mother and father righted themselves and began to walk. The young girl stood by her brother's side and rubbed his back as he wiped tears from his face. I noticed the familiar feeling of frost spreading through my veins. I looked down at my daughter, who was blissfully unaware of what had just transpired. "Honey, I think that I am going to reward you with something other than a toy. Maybe we should go to the park later." She looked up at me and smiled, and I smiled back.

I walked down the aisle where the family had been standing and threw two of the dolls into the cart. I walked to the front of the store and placed my items on the first checkout lane that was empty and purchased everything I had grabbed. After loading up my car, my daughter and I sat there and watched the front door of the store from our respective seats. I highly doubt that she was watching like I was, but it did seem like a nice bonding moment. She got to see a bit more of her father that day.

After maybe half an hour, the family exited and made their way to their large and fancy SUV. They got loaded up and began to drive, at which point I followed. I had not practiced the art of tailing another person, but it seemed relatively simple. In the parking lot, I ensured there was one car between me and them. While driving on the road, I kept a safe distance of about thirty to fifty feet. My car was rather inconspicuous, so they had no real logical reason to be worried if they noticed me. They also gave no indication that they had.

Finally, their SUV pulled into a driveway. I took a mental note of the address and continued to drive down the street, heading toward the park. Something about the scene and the feeling I was experiencing put me in the mood to share and talk about my thoughts.

"Listen young lady, during your life I am going to give you a lot of lessons about what is right and wrong. But there are always exceptions to the rules. Some people are bad people, and bad people deserve consequences."

She babbled in her somewhat coherent toddler talk that I had still not perfected the skill of deciphering.

"Exactly. What you said. Those people were bad people. They made your dad very angry, and now Dad is going to have to do something with that anger. But don't worry, because Dad knows what to do."

As I continued the drive, she responded back in her gibberish. I only made out two words: "bad people."

My wife had planned a girls' weekend that was supposed to take place two weeks after the scene in the grocery store. She and some friends were going to a concert or something, but I was unable to take time off from work. We had arranged it so that she could drop our daughter off with my wife's parents for the weekend to allow her time away and me some time to myself. She had made comments about how much she appreciated my efforts around the house and my attentiveness to her and our daughter's needs, but she expressed worry about my lack of self-care. She told me that she wanted me to take the weekend to unwind and relax, to do something that was just for me. When she first said this while planning the trip, I was at a loss as to what that would be. Now, I had a plan.

Friday morning, my wife packed up clothes for our daughter, kissed me goodbye, and left to drop her off and go enjoy her weekend. I went to work and saw my patients as normal. It was a decent enough day, and I easily stayed focused on my tasks. When I finished, I went home to make dinner. I had cooked some pork schnitzel with mashed potatoes and asparagus (there's no justification to eat like a slob as an adult just because there's no supervision). I watched a movie while I ate, enjoying the silence and lack of required conversational etiquette.

When night was upon me, I got dressed in a pair of black work pants that I kept in case I needed to do some form of labor that was likely to leave stains, as well as a black long-sleeve shirt that I'd bought to replace the one I had ruined during my last encounter with the nurse. I remember thinking that I should just buy these in bulk if this hobby continued.

I didn't need any tools or equipment; I could make do with whatever the family had in their house. I grabbed both dolls that I had hidden under some luggage in my closet.

I hadn't given much thought to what I would do. I just knew I was going to pay them a visit, and it would not be a kind one. Every time I thought of that day in the store, I felt the same chill spread through me. However, I didn't plan some elaborate scene where I would teach them about the wrongs in their parenting choices. I just wanted to hurt them.

I waited until a little past midnight and drove back to the address I had spent days ensuring I memorized. I had been so busy helping around the house, I didn't have time to survey their behavior and calculate the best time for my entrance. I assumed the middle of the night would be as good a time as any. I mimicked similar behaviors as I had in the past and parked several blocks down. From there, I walked to their house, steering clear of any streetlamp light in case some nosy neighbor was outside. I carried the two dolls in a small black backpack that I kept in my car.

Their SUV was parked in the driveway, and all the lights in the house were off. I tried the front door in case they were so stupid as to leave it unlocked, but they hadn't been.

I walked toward the back and jumped the chain-link fence that bordered their property. The back door was sliding glass that was also locked, but that was only a false sense of security.

I have learned a lot of skills unintentionally during my life. Shortly after we first moved into my house, our sliding door had gotten a large crack in it from a bird that apparently was tired of existence. I chose to replace it on my own, saving us the money of hiring someone else to do a job that I was certain I was capable of. I discovered that it was rather easy to get a sliding door off its tracks with a little patience and an object that could pry it up. Lucky for me, I always carried a multi-tool in case of emergencies.

I jammed the large flat-head attachment in between the frame and door and began trying to dislodge the door. It took the better part of fifteen minutes before I felt it come loose. The difficulty was remaining quiet while I did so. With the door off the tracks enough, it created a gap through which I could use the same multitool to slowly slide the hook lock up and provide me with access to enter through.

I gave myself a tour of their home, moving with intention and caution. I realized it was good they didn't have pets. I would have to consider that moving forward.

The house was very nice. It was perfectly clean. There were no dishes in the sink or cups on the counter. The living room had two boxes, one pink and one blue. All the toys were neatly placed into the boxes, with not a single building block on the floor. It was quite an impressive and immaculate sight.

I walked to the door that I could logically deduce led into the garage. The tools were perfectly placed on some type of peg board, and the pink and purple yoga equipment lay neatly on the opposing side of the garage.

I thought to myself how interesting it was that they didn't just distinguish between gender of family members with color and purpose, but also created physical divides between each gender's belongings. God forbid the toys in the living room be placed in a single box, or that mother and father blend their equipment on one side of the garage. Everything had to be in its place, and everything had to be separated.

I looked at the tools that were available to me and treated it like trick-or-treat. Grab whatever catches my eye in the bucket and make the best use of it later. I picked up a rope, which I assumed I would use to tie them up, a hammer for who knows what purpose, and a box cutter because why not? I made my way back into the house holding my newly acquired equipment and headed for the hallway that I had only glanced down before. It was decorated with nice family photos, each one showing a different assortment of family members, each with big smiles and eyes that betrayed the authenticity of the moment. Two of the doors had a sign hanging at eye level, one blue and one pink, with the names of the current inhabitants.

Shit.

Somehow, I hadn't connected the dots that the children would be in the house and would most likely wake up. I had no desire to subject two small children to the sight of violence, plus I figured if they saw my face, I would have to kill them as well. They didn't give me that urge, so I was opposed to the idea of taking it so far. My mind ran through ideas, and I finally decided that I would tie the rope I had grabbed to one door handle and then tie it to the other door's handle. This way, if they woke up and tried to open the door, there wouldn't be enough slack to allow them an exit, and I could ensure they were both kept away from what was to happen soon.

I lacked my normal confidence in this decision, but I figured it was the most effective way without literally nailing their doors shut. And as my past had proved, fire will make quick work of a person if they can't escape. If I nailed the doors shut, and something unexpected occurred, then I would again be the cause of unintended collateral damage.

I took a deep breath once I was satisfied with my rope idea, then gathered myself and approached the third door in the hallway. I placed my backpack on the floor so it wouldn't encumber me or get blood on it. I liked that bag.

I slowly opened the door, ensuring that it didn't even squeak. There was mother and father, lying in bed, with their backs to each other. *How sad that a home can be so lacking in love that you don't even touch your spouse in your sleep*, I thought to myself. It was an unnecessary judgment, because I had no way of knowing if it was true, but it was still funny in my head.

I had no clue what I was going to do. I was still inexperienced at that point. Should I wake them up by speaking? Should I get close and threaten them, brandishing the box cutter? Should I kill one while they slept so the other would be in shock and less likely to think logically? I had never realized how much work went into taking someone's life. There were so many decisions and so many options. It was like planning a family vacation—I knew there must be a correct way to go about it, but I was just guessing.

I walked to the bed and decided to let instinct guide me. The entire purpose of this experiment was to gauge my instincts, so why fight it? I raised the hammer over my head and brought it down hard into the wife's jaw. It made contact with her face, with a loud thud and the cracking of her jawbone. She woke immediately and grabbed the point of impact. Her husband shot up and saw me standing there, hammer in hand.

I spoke in a hushed and aggressive tone: "Don't move or make a sound and you might get to walk away from this." That wasn't technically a lie in my opinion. I didn't know how this night would end for sure. But I knew that if they started screaming, I would start swinging.

They both froze. The wife, still lying on her back, stared up at me, tears in her eyes, clutching her jaw. The husband remained in an odd, half-seated position, his eyes a mix of rage and fear. His posture looked as if he were preparing to either attack me or make a run for the door. Not once did his glance shift to see if his wife was okay.

He spoke up but kept it quiet. "What do you want? Get out of my house."

What did I want? Well, I couldn't answer that question honestly. I don't like lying to direct questions, but I felt it was necessary. "I want to talk to you. So, answer my questions and we can finish this up quick." My heart was racing. This was new to me. I had full control over these people, and the excitement of the whole situation filled me like a warm drink on a cold night.

"You mangled my wife's face. Fuck you, asshole.

I'm not having a conversation with you." I could tell he wanted to throttle me. I didn't understand immediately, but a small smile crept onto my face. Only later did I realize the smile came from appreciating how helpless and powerless he must have felt. Just as helpless and powerless as a child getting slapped in the face for asking for a toy.

The wife reached out and placed her hand on her husband's arm. She was looking at him and not me. Interesting. Her face appeared to be a mix of fear and concern, but all of that was aimed at her husband. She didn't utter a word, but I wasn't sure she was able to with that injury to her jaw. His demeanor softened a bit, but it was obvious he was staying ready to act if given the opportunity. "Say what you need to, then get the hell out," he spoke through gritted teeth.

Once again, I hadn't thought about this very much at all. I wanted to say something. Hurting them without saying anything seemed too impersonal, and honestly a bit disrespectful. I didn't want this to be an intimate act, but I did want them to know that this wasn't a random choice. They were selected purposefully; it was important to me they knew that. I stood there silently and stared at them. The wife was beginning to inch closer to the other side of the bed, but when she saw me look at her, she stopped. The husband stared daggers at me before speaking up again. "What? I thought you wanted to talk. If you want a fight, I can give that to you also."

I'm not sure if he thought his threats would intimidate me or if he was trying to somehow bolster his own sense of control. He seemed like the type that was used to being in control, being the most dominant person in the room. Finally, I knew what I wanted to say.

"What are your kids' names?" I spoke softly, releasing the aggression for a moment.

He looked puzzled. "What?"

"Your children. The ones I saw you with at the store. What are their names?"

"Screw you, psycho. Why do you want to know?"

I let silence hang in the air for just a few seconds. "I find it interesting that you have threatened me, cussed at me, told me to leave, but at no point have you asked if your kids are okay or even alive. I want to know if you love them enough to even remember their names."

This statement obviously took him by surprise. He told me their names. He paused before speaking again. "I was worried about them. I wanted you out so I could check on them."

Now, I was amused. "Oh, you were worried. So worried that you got aggressive with the man with the weapon. I could have killed you both and then done whatever I wanted with those children, and you wouldn't be alive to protect them. Did you really think antagonizing me would help them? Or was it to cater to your ego?"

His anger quickly returned. "This isn't about my ego asshole. I want you out of my house, now."

"Fair enough. Then answer one more question honestly, and I will just leave. Deal?" I didn't know how much truth there was in that statement. I wasn't opposed to leaving if I found that my previous appraisal of the family was incorrect. I also wanted to kill them, though.

"Get on it with it then." His challenge was issued with confidence. He shifted his body to brace himself for the question, moving closer to me. Maybe he was planning an attack, or maybe he didn't like feeling inferior. Either way, I made no move to discourage it. His wife stayed frozen on her side of the bed, blood starting to trickle from between the fingers clutching her mouth and jaw.

"What will you do if your son is gay?" The question hung in the air for almost a full minute. Both he and his wife looked confused. I truly wanted to know the answer. I hadn't ever given much thought to sexuality, because I thought it was an inane topic to get worked up over. However, at that moment, the sight of him admonishing his child for feminine behavior bothered me. I related to the child, because of all the times people treated me poorly for being different.

"I don't know. I guess I would just deal with it." He stammered over the words. His response lacked confidence, and he shifted with discomfort.

"I didn't say guess an answer. I said tell me your answer. Try again with no guessing."

Now seeming both irritated and uncomfortable, he said, "I'll be fine with it. But he's not."

I wanted to egg him on. "He's not what?"

Full confidence returned to his body. He looked me straight in the eyes and spoke. "A fa—"

I swung with the hammer and smashed it into the side of his head. Blood shot across the bed and splattered over the wife. She panicked and attempted to throw herself from the far side. I grabbed her ankle while simultaneously dropping the hammer to the ground. I gripped her leg tight with one hand and found the box cutter in my pocket with the other. The blade extended with several clicks, right before I dragged it across the back of her ankle. It sank in deep and easily glided through the muscle and fiber of her Achilles. She attempted to let out a scream, but it had to fight past her clenched and frozen jaw. It sounded more like a groan.

I jerked her leg hard and pulled her toward me so that I could put my hand over her mouth. The pain in her jaw must have been intense as I clenched my hand around it; I watched as she started to lose consciousness. Before she could, I slid the blade of the box cutter across her throat. Blood shot up and painted my face. Her eyes went lifeless and her body went limp.

She slid off the mattress once I released her. Her husband was unconscious from the blow to his skull, but that didn't stop me from doing what I came to do. I moved with expert precision as I rolled him over onto his back and began stabbing into his abdomen repeatedly. I don't remember if he woke up during the process or not; I was far too entranced in what I was doing. That feeling of release started to wash over me, and I entered euphoria once again.

Once my task was completed, I stepped back to take stock of my work. The husband lay on the bed spread-eagle in his boxers. Multiple wounds in his stomach glistened in the minimal light from the moon outside. The wife leaned against the bed, her legs under her, like crumpled trash discarded. I didn't feel pride or fulfillment, just that same sweet relief of stress. Red stains covered the carpets and sheets, and sprays of blood had reached the headboard at some point.

I wiped some of the blood from my face with the sleeve of my shirt and turned to leave. Once I exited the bedroom, I kneeled to get into my backpack. I grabbed both dolls from it and placed one in front of each of the children's bedrooms. There was blood on the boxes from my gloves, but I doubted that would be the most traumatic discovery in the next twelve hours. I closed the parents' door, grabbed my bag, cut the rope tying the two doors together with the same box cutter, and left out the front.

After the clothes, tools, and gloves were burned in the fire, I returned home and took a shower. The rest of the weekend was spent cleaning up the house and preparing for my family's return. My self-care had been successful and fully accomplished on the first night.

14

CHOICE

I have always had specific reasons for choosing my victims. I see something in them that sparks an urge. However, I am not blaming them for my decisions. My victims all choose to be who they want to be, and they have every right to do so. And I make the choice to harm them. They have a behavior; I have a reaction. I then choose to act on that emotional reaction.

Choice is a funny thing. We all make countless choices every single day. Each of those choices carries with it some level of risk for negative consequences. So why do so many people look to blame other people for the consequences they face? You made a choice that put you in a situation. It is unreasonable to place the entirety of fault on someone else because there was a negative outcome.

I think it starts with parents. We hear parents

making excuses and platitudes all the time to remove potential guilt from their seed: "Boys will be boys"; "They're just a kid—how could they know better?"; or "It isn't her fault, she's the girl." No. Just no. The child made a decision. If they didn't know better, there should be consequences, so the lesson is not soon forgotten.

When I lost my first job because I lost my temper and decided to act on it, it wasn't testosterone's fault. "Boys will be boys" is one of the worst excuses—we use it in almost no other scenario that I can think of. If a dog releases its bladder on the carpet, we don't say "dogs will be dogs." We put its nose in the mess, smack it on the butt, and then put it outside.

Everyone is responsible for their own actions and nothing more. If someone is disrespectful, you can choose to hit them, choose to tell them to shut up, or choose to walk away. Their decision to be disrespectful is not in your control, and they cannot control how you respond to them. By being disrespectful, they have chosen to accept whatever consequences are conceivable for that behavior. The person who chooses to hit the disrespectful individual chooses to accept the consequences for physical violence. Don't blame your choice on the target when there are other choices.

Some choices are so difficult that trying to make them is nearly impossible. The only option that I have that I've never explored is for me to stop killing altogether. It is like an addiction. Simply stopping would not be sustainable for me. Asking someone addicted to heroin to "just stop" is like asking a teenager to "just not use the internet." It is technically an option on the table, but one that would require such great effort that I would most likely fail. Addiction can be overcome, but usually with some form of help or support. I don't have any available support group for serial killers. Getting mental health assistance would likely have the same result as turning myself in.

The only thing that is guaranteed to us as humans is choice, and people want to sacrifice that so that they can feel innocent. I think it is a large reason our society is the cesspool that it is. Not because people choose to be polyamorous, homosexual, Republicans, etc. It is because other people choose to use those decisions as justification to act like horrible human beings, while simultaneously blaming the targets of their hate. I kill people because I choose to. I don't need to justify it.

15

This was an odd time in my life. I had killed multiple people now, and I had already spent the necessary time reflecting on these urges after my first kill. Nothing changed with this most recent couple. I still felt no shame, no guilt, no regret. Everything had gone according to plan. I had been curious whether the lack of exposure to investigating officials would change my response to this incident or not. With the first woman, I spoke with the police directly and was allowed to set up a sort of scapegoat for myself. Now, I was solely reliant on the potential incompetence of whomever would be investigating if I wanted to ensure my freedom. Injecting myself into the investigation would have seemed suspicious.

I watched the reports with a sense of comfort and calm whenever they appeared on the news. *Gristly Homicide of Local Parents. Upstanding Citizens Brutally Murdered.* Etc. Etc.

The headlines were laughable. What was so up-standing about those two? The public eye is everywhere but does not perceive with any level of scrutiny. Did that make me a hypocrite, to be so judgmental of them? I didn't care if I was. They had a chance to stop me, to answer my questions honestly, but instead they only covered for themselves. They both prioritized protecting themselves over the other people in the house. The husband chose to try to aggravate their attacker. If I were in a similar situation, I would absolutely be most focused on ending the invader's life. But I wouldn't merely attempt to intimidate and display dominance. I would kill the invader quickly and effectively, so as to ensure the safety of my family.

As I watched the reporters and news anchors, I realized that there was very little I would be able to do if forensic evidence was discovered. Science has come a long way, and even the most miniscule hair could lead to my arrest. I had considered the advantages of killing only those people that I had no connection to, because there would be no logical string connecting the victim and myself. However, the downside was that I had no way of explaining my presence in a murder victim's home. I could always claim that I had run into the victim in some public setting, remaining ambiguous enough due to a failure in memory recall, thus explaining the possibility of picking up some form of physical evidence.

I started to consider other methods of ensuring my continued safety, as if I had already decided that this was the path I was meant to walk.

My wife had seen me watching the different reports on the incident and decided to join me one
night. She watched about ten to fifteen minutes of the
journalists describing the scene of the murder and discussing the future of the now-orphaned children.
"Wow. That is absolutely horrible. I can't believe that
this happened in our city. You really never feel unsafe
when you watch these things?" She gave me a look of
mild fear and uneasiness.

What an interesting question. Somehow, up to this
moment, I hadn't considered how my actions would
eventually affect my own family. Better yet, how I
would respond to questions about the events. She was
right, it was a horrible scene. Those parents being allowed to raise two children, traumatize them, and then
continue a path of generational trauma would have
been much worse, though.

That response was clearly inappropriate—it would
expose that I had knowledge of the family. I looked at
her calmly and replied, "No, not really. I guess I don't
think of this happening to me. We keep our doors
locked, and I think I can protect us if it was needed."

My wife was quick with her response. "Yeah. But
you're a psychiatrist. You work with people that have
these types of thoughts and urges, right? You don't
ever wonder what if one of them follows you home?"

Again, a very fair question. It was moments like
this that I was reassured about my reasons for marry-
ing this woman. She was very intelligent and knew
how to challenge me, even if it was unintentional. If
only I could tell her the truth, then she wouldn't need

to be nervous. *Honey, you don't need to be scared. I killed those people, and I have no desire to harm you in any way. So relax.*

"Nope, never thought about it. I guess if it happened, I would just have to stop them before they hurt you." I flashed her a reassuring and cocky smile, then planted a light kiss on her forehead, as if communicating that anyone who would dare try something like that would be in far greater danger than we were. She chuckled and cuddled into my arm. She took my comment as a joke. If only she knew that it was the most honest thing I had ever said to her.

I went through the next few weeks feeling very calm and relaxed. It was like I was walking on air. I was no longer trying to wrestle with myself in deciding if I would ever act on these urges again or not. I knew I would. My plan was to go through my days as if everything was normal; if someone sparked that urge, then I would quench my thirst again.

I continued to spend my day-to-day life in the comfortable routine that allowed me to survive in this society. I went to work, came home and played with my daughter, and then spent time with my wife before bed. I was happy with this routine because it was simple and provided me adequate and acceptable justification for my lack of social interaction.

All of that was somewhat ruined when I arrived home one day.

I walked in, and my daughter ran up to me to say hello. She was somewhat verbal (as verbal as any toddler could be) and mobile. As I walked in, I saw my wife sitting at the dining room table with an odd look on her face. I could see hints of fear and concern, but not so intense that she appeared panicked. "Hi. How was your day?" I asked her, hoping to probe further into her mood without directly calling her out.

"It was pretty good. A lot of things happened. Why don't you go get changed and everything, and we can talk about our days after that?" Her response was lousy with failed deception, a poor attempt to avoid a topic she was obviously not prepared to speak about. I didn't challenge her any further. If she didn't want to talk about it, that was less stress on me and I could relax for the night.

I walked into my room and removed the horribly uncomfortable business attire I was required to wear with my status as a professional. As I walked into the restroom to relieve myself, I saw something sitting on the counter next to our sink.

I am not an unintelligent man. As I looked at this small piece of plastic, my mind couldn't process what I was seeing, though. I refused to touch it, as if it was some kind of venomous animal, poised to strike. Even from a distance, I could see the two small blue lines. Frustration spread through my body. It felt like every time I started to gain a modicum of control in my life, something else would come around to upset the balance.

A myriad of thoughts ran through my mind as I stared, the pressure of future stressors already starting to set in. I would have to try and bond with more people. I would have to go through the emotional rollercoaster of the nine months of parasitic growth. If I believed in any type of deity, I would have prayed that this was a mistake. Images of addressing this problem appeared and disappeared quickly, all of them violent and harming one of the few people I had no desire to harm. I took a deep breath and resigned myself to the reality that none of those options were feasible or realistic if I wanted to continue my way of life. I took a deep breath and looked in the mirror. I watched my reflection as I practiced my look of shock and joy before stepping out and performing it in front of her.

Seventeen. I killed seventeen people between the ages of thirty-seven and thirty-nine. This brought my total of intentional victims (so not including the ones in the first fire when I was younger) to twenty people. The stress of another pregnancy, the birth of twins (one boy and a second girl), and continuing to function as an adult in society was overwhelming at the best of times and completely crushing at the worst. The seventeen that I chose were all people that fit my criteria for people that had chosen to forfeit their right to life by being insufferable. Regardless of the stress that bore down on my shoulders, I refused to sacrifice my own guidelines for a "quick fix."

The first two happened within two weeks of discovering my wife's pregnancy: two men that I saw harassing a young woman at a bar. I'd opted to stop in for a quick drink one Saturday evening without any intention of violence. I typically struggle with witnessing this type of behavior; lewd and brazen sexual harassment always seemed to me to reflect an infuriating sense of entitlement and grandiosity. I intervened on behalf of the young woman by approaching the men and placing one hand on each of their shoulders to feel for any potential movement toward me or the girl.

I looked at them both and stated, "Guys, you don't want to waste your time on such a prude. I have some friends coming in the next hour, and there will be some girls that I can introduce you to." The men were already somewhat intoxicated and saw the logic in my statement. The woman left hastily while mouthing *Thank you*.

I sat with the men for the next hour and got them as drunk as possible through manipulation and gaslighting. It isn't actually as hard as most people would expect, especially with men like this. I challenged their masculinity and pitted them against each other to turn a night of consumption into competition. I told them that I was choosing to maintain a level of sobriety so that I could talk them up to my friends. They were so engrossed in their own drinking competition that they didn't even seem to notice.

After the hour passed, I faked receiving a phone call and informed them that "my friends were at a campsite not far from here, and their car won't start. But they invited me, and I convinced them to let you come along to meet the girls." The severely inebriated pair jumped at the possibility of getting laid, almost pushing each other over to get to my car. I drove them out to the woods, as promised, and proceeded to bash both over the head repeatedly with a tire iron. In an attempt at a sick joke, which was probably lost on whomever discovered the bodies, I stripped them of their clothes and belongings before positioning their corpses in a sexual position. I then cleaned any possible fingerprints off the weapon and sodomized one of the men with it to complete the scene. I was somewhat annoyed at first that I would have to eventually buy a new tire iron, but it was covered in blood and hair anyway.

Based on news reports, the police assumed it was either gay bashing turned fatal, or that the men were sharing a sexual partner that became violent. Either way, I was in the clear.

After them, there was a family of five. A mother, father, two adolescent sons, and one adult daughter. The family had been making a name for themselves in local social media groups about the issue of their neighborhood "taking a turn for the worse" when people of different "ethnic backgrounds" started buying houses. I would normally not care too deeply about the opinions or biases of others, but seeing signs, news reports, and social media posts was beginning to infringe on my sense of peace. I may be evil, but I do not encourage others to agree with my thoughts. They were recruiting for their special brand of evil.

Breaking into their house was a real pain. Apparently, the presence of individuals with more melanin requires more advanced security systems. I posed as an evening visitor who was coming over to beg for an opportunity to "assist the cause." I spoke with the mother and father for possibly the worst three hours of my life and feigned intoxication while asking to sleep on their couch afterward, as if four beers were enough to impair me that greatly. They gladly welcomed a "like-minded" person to stay. Truly morons.

I entered the adult daughter's bedroom first, because it was closest to the living room that I'd been offered as a sleeping area. She hadn't done anything particularly horrible to me and hadn't spoken as loudly as her parents did. However, she also continued to benefit from the wealth of hate-mongers, so I took my knife and pushed it quickly into her heart while using my other hand to cover her mouth and hold her down until she sank back into sleep.

I had some misgivings about killing minors at first. When I entered the first one's room, after cutting both of his parents' throats and removing their tongues to later nail to their door, I saw a variety of thinly veiled racist propaganda posters covering his walls and a copy of *Mein Kampf* on his bookshelf. The misgivings immediately faded. Not as shockingly as I would have liked, killing the two minors was just as easy as killing the parents.

I suppose a well-adjusted individual would have felt guilt about the police's primary theory in this case. They assumed that some minority group that took offense to their "political stance" came in and murdered them. The police said that the tongues were the greatest clue, because it most likely represented an individual attempting to "stop them from spewing lies about other races." I had in fact cut out their tongues because the conversation with them irked me to my very core. I didn't intend for the detectives to blame people that had already been victimized by this family's hate. Oh well. C'est la vie.

After the family was the lesbian couple. I didn't have any strong, or even existing, opinions about the homosexual population. I often saw the couple in the morning while I got my cup of coffee. They would be sitting at a small table outside in their thrift store purchases and "bohemian chique" wardrobe.

I had a few run-ins with them over time. The first was on a morning where one of the women was wearing a particularly odd outfit, which included a crocheted hat and a shawl that looked like a rainbow threw up on it. I didn't realize, but I was staring at her, considering what would inspire a person to dress in such an attention-grabbing and flamboyant style. She noticed the attention I was giving to her and her partner, quickly returning an angry glare. I didn't blame her. I was being rude by staring, so I returned to my previous task by entering the coffee shop.

As I walked through the door, I heard her shout. "Get a good look?"

I chose not to acknowledge her. The question seemed rhetorical, and interacting with her wouldn't benefit me. I didn't want to argue with a stranger about their odd style of dress.

A few weeks after that, I was walking out after making my purchase. The couple were sitting at their usual table. I had made sure to not give them any more uninvited attention. They were weird. I didn't understand. Nothing more to examine. However, as I was walking out, a truck driving down the road slowed down and the driver yelled dykes as he passed. I saw the situation play out and I couldn't help but chuckle to myself. I didn't find the derogatory comment funny. I thought it was humorous that someone was so bothered by two people sharing a coffee together that he needed to shout his disapproval as he passed. How is that not pitiful and humorous?

Regardless of my reason for laughing, the girls didn't appreciate my reaction. As I turned to walk toward my car, one of them yelled at me. "You think that's funny, fascist?"

I paused. I understood why she was upset. She thought that I found the harassment of them funny. I could've stopped and explained myself, but I was more upset that she'd made an assumption about me. I turned toward her and calmly responded, "Yes. I do." Then I left.

I planned to let it be. We'd had two encounters that were poisoned by miscommunication, and I didn't think it required any follow-up. We could ignore each other and dislike each other from a distance. But one day I walked out of the coffee shop to see dozens of rainbow stickers covering the majority of my car. It took me forty-five minutes to remove them all, and then another hour of washing to remove the adhesive residue that remained. They were now officially wasting my time. I value my time and didn't appreciate it being wasted on this couple's ignorance and assumptions. They thought they had the right to do what they wanted since they saw me as some kind of biased homophobe. More importantly, that was my car. My property. My property is an extension of me. Defacing my property is akin to defacing my body.

I refused to let the indiscretion go.

Again, it was not all that difficult. I rented a car since they were so familiar with my own, parked away from the coffee shop one morning, and followed them back to their home. My anger and irritation at having my urges tested for something so insignificant was intense. I rang their doorbell and asked if I could come in to speak about the vandalism of my car. They refused at first, but when I made a comment about notifying the police and filing a civil suit against them for property damage, they reluctantly agreed to "talk it out like adults." The fear of public shame and financial retribution is powerful for many.

After I smashed one of them in the face with an ash tray that was sitting next to their sofa, the concussion rendering her unable to gather the sense to scream out, I suffocated the other with a pillow. I finished my work with the first by repeatedly striking her with the ash tray. It was strong and good quality, as evidenced by the ease with which I fractured and crushed parts of her skull.

This was the first time I had killed someone midday. Before, I'd always attempted to do my work at night as a security measure against being discovered.

There were several more after them. A contractor that a client had warned me was intentionally building subpar housing to sell at maximum profit. A polyamorous triad that had annoyed me in a restaurant after making a large-scale scene about how beautiful their nonstandard relationship was (no one had asked them and it was just annoying). Then another family of four that were boycotting a local private school for allowing openly gay students to attend classes with their children. I'm still not positive why I felt an urge to kill the children in that situation. I think it was simply the thought that they had already been poisoned by their parents' ignorance and audacity.

Seventeen bodies in three years. Twenty intentional bodies in my adulthood. Twenty-three bodies in total in my lifetime. I never took the time to contemplate if my increasing frequency was a sign of negative events yet to come. I was spending more time thinking about killing, which led to me neglecting my wife and three small children.

I did, however, realize the folly in how I went about my actions when watching a news report about the final family.

A reporter was addressing the law enforcement and asked, "Sir, do you think that there is some connection between this most recently family and the family from three years ago? Both families were being covered in the media when they were murdered, and both crime scenes contain high levels of brutality. Have the police explored this possibility?"

What an absurd question. Three years is equal to 1,095 days. Two separate families in that time frame seemed like a far stretch. On average, the city had one hundred homicides per year. My measly body count shouldn't have registered.

My assumption was that the reporter was trying to

create some sensationalized news in order to posit that a serial killer or vigilante might be on the loose. Referring to the brutality was a tactic to try and exacerbate the news. I didn't grasp that it was somehow drastically different for a man to shoot his neighbor versus someone being beaten and removing two parents' tongues. They were both murders. It didn't matter that the reporter was right; she had no evidence to lead her to that conclusion.

The chief said, "We have noticed the similarities between both families, the media attention they were receiving, and the manner in which they were murdered. We have considered investigating them as connected, but I cannot share any further details at this time."

Shit. I hadn't thought about them connecting my motive between those two families. I had continued to look at the large picture and how much time had passed. But both families had been open about hatred toward a minority group and were gaining media popularity. Both families were killed in their homes at night with the primary weapon being a blade. I screwed up. If they were able to connect the two families, could they somehow find other breadcrumbs that would connect them to the other murders?

I considered quitting altogether. The police had sufficient evidence to start an investigation that could potentially narrow their suspects. I knew that the chances of them identifying me were still highly unlikely, but the likelihood had increased with that connection.

Quitting didn't seem appealing. My twins were walking and talking, and my first was starting school.

My stress continued to grow. I needed to find a new method of approaching these behaviors to protect myself. Leaving bodies behind was problematic, because it was immediately obvious to investigators that it was murder. Killing people at the height of their infamy was also rather indicative of motive, thus creating an easier connection between crimes. However, it was difficult to consider being set off by a person and then waiting six months or a year to do something about it. I went to the mental drawing board and reconsidered every aspect of my approach so that I could continue to feel safe.

I took a break for several months to provide myself with sufficient time to recalculate my methodology and help dissuade police. I focused more on my work and my family during this time. I found that I was starting to bond more with my children during this period, even beginning to feel a level of affection to them. I struggle to say it was paternal love, because it looked so much different from how other parents loved their children. I think it might best be described as possessiveness. They were my children and therefore unique and special to me.

I started to notice a tension growing between my wife and me. Through numerous conversations, it became clear that she was feeling ignored because of the time I spent at my office. I apologized and told her that I would take some time off work to help more around the house. This statement was technically already true;

I was going to take a break. My biggest mistake was in offering to show the authenticity of my affection by agreeing to accompany her in her personal life so that I could get to know her even better. I didn't think that this would lead to my return to killing, but alas, I have never been capable of predicting the future.

I first assisted my wife with grocery shopping, and that progressed to standing by her side at social gatherings with her friends. These were unfathomably frustrating tasks. It took an incredible amount of energy masking as the dutiful and perfect husband. My wife would shower me with praise afterward for being so amazing, and apparently, I earned multiple statements of admiration from her other married friends. Eventually, we even had to host a small gathering with her friends. Strangers. A group of strangers. In my house and requiring my attention.

All of this was harsh, but it was bearable for her sake. I didn't want to lose her, and if being social was necessary, I could do it. I would have never guessed that a smaller event with only one of her friends would push me past my limits.

My wife approached me one morning, "Honey, I'm taking the kids to my friend's house for lunch today. I thought it would be nice for you to have some time to yourself."

She wasn't wrong. Some time to myself would have been amazing. But my hubris got the better of me, and I thought it would earn me extra points and greater benefits later if I offered to accompany her to the gathering that she'd designed to give me freedom.

"I really appreciate that, but I don't need it right now. I've enjoyed all of this time together, and it would be nice to meet one of your friends in a more personal setting." All of that was lies, but if I could deal with up to ten adults and their children, I could deal with just one or two, right?

She walked up to me and placed her palms on my chest before rising on her toes to offer a kiss. She kissed me deeply, let out a soft moan as our lips parted, and quietly said, "How did I get so lucky to have a husband like you?"

I stared into her eyes before leaning down and kissing her cheek. I whispered in her ear, "I'm the lucky one here. I get to try and be the best husband for an already perfect woman." We hugged as she breathed in my scent and I breathed in hers. I never understood why she would do that. I knew that I did it; it was something I did as a child and had continued into my adulthood. A person's scent can tell you a great deal about who they are. It tells you about their hygiene, their habits, and who they have been around. If a person's scent changes, it means that their routine has changed. I wonder if she did it for the same reason, but I somehow doubt it.

We got the kids ready and packed a few toys for my first daughter. The two toddlers were pretty easy, since all of their toys strapped on to the handles of their car seats. We got into the car and drove to her friend's house. On the way, my wife filled me in on the pertinent information about this individual. She was a single mother of two children, a twelve-year-old boy and a ten-year-old girl. Each child had a different father whom she had divorced. She worked in human resources or some other mundane field that seemed helpful on the surface but was actually rather pointless. My wife told me that her kids were a bit rambunctious because they were being a raised by a single mother, and that their mother could be a handful because she had been through so much.

I was confused as I listened to her talk, because it seemed like this lady had very little in common with my wife. I asked her where they'd met, and my wife explained that they'd met at my first daughter's gymnastics gym. The woman's daughter did gymnastics there as well, so they started talking while waiting for classes to end. I thought it was odd to form a friendship with someone simply because you both have children with similar interests, but I kept the thought to myself.

As we pulled into the driveway of this woman's home, I put my car into park and my wife added, "Please. She is my friend. I know she can be a bit much, but she's actually a good person. Just don't judge her too harshly."

Her eyes were pleading with me. I sat confused for a moment. The sound of my oldest daughter's tablet as she matched same-colored balloons or candy or whatever and as they flew away into her point box was the only noise. I looked at my wife and understood that for one reason or another, she wanted me to approve of this person and not take any actions that would jeopardize their friendship. "I understand. I don't plan to judge her at all. You trust her, and that is more than enough for me." I released my seatbelt and leaned forward to give her a quick kiss. She smiled back at me and climbed out of the car, and we began to unload our three children, the diaper bags, and the portable crib device that was required anytime we would be somewhere for a potentially extended stay.

My wife rang the doorbell, and we were greeted by a very attractive middle-aged blond woman. Her body was toned and somewhat muscular, displayed by her summer dress, showing obvious hints of her active gym life and the value she placed on fitness and appearance. Every physical attribute that would attract a potential mate was in perfect proportion, and so my mind began to wonder what had caused both of her marriages to dissolve. Maybe they were neglectful and abusive, or maybe she was more than merely high maintenance.

We were ushered in, and introductions were made between the adults and children. The single mother's son was still somewhat small for his age, and he wore his dirty-blond hair intentionally messy. His clothes were somewhat baggy. His bright orange shirt depicted some skateboarder doing a trick where he grabbed his board, forever suspended in that pose on the horrendously ugly background. The daughter had similar hair, and her entire wardrobe and demeanor gave the impression of meekness and innocence. It became evident quickly that my daughter was enamored with the older girl and wanted to know everything about her.

The three older children shuffled off to another room while the toddlers stayed glued to me mostly. My wife and the single mother quickly began chatting, their giggles sounding out from the conversation. I opted to sit at the dining room table, and they sat in chairs on the opposite side of the table as me. My toddlers were trying to show me neat things they were finding around the house, requiring me to express shock and enjoyment while also quickly removing the items from their grasp as they explored. The three older kids would run in occasionally and share some banal fact that I would nod my head at as if it were the most interesting thing I had heard that day.

I watched as the kids played and noticed that these two strange children behaved in several somewhat questionable ways. The older brother would push his sister, and the sister would occasionally stick her middle finger in his face. Profanity doesn't bother me much. What did bother me was the woman speaking with my wife, who either disregarded these actions because she didn't think they were important enough to address, or paid so little attention to her children that she didn't even notice it.

I put my concerns to the side and continued to focus on my toddlers while the women continued to yap on about topics that couldn't have sparked my interest if they included flint and steel. At one point I stood up to grab myself some snacks from the kitchen, which was adjacent to the dining room. I found the woman's son standing in the kitchen mindlessly gnawing at a cookie, and his attention became directed at me as I made my way to the refrigerator to grab something off a fruit tray that had previously been offered to me.

"So that's your wife in there?" the boy said from

behind me. He sounded arrogant and mischievous, instead of the confused and innocent tone I was accustomed to with my own oldest.

"Yes." I pulled the tray out and placed it on the counter. I pulled the clear plastic lid off of it, and it made the loud cracking noises that those store-bought containers always do.

"She's really hot. You aren't good looking enough for her." I looked at his face and immediately recognized the smug look as a signal that he was attempting to test me. I wasn't angry or irritated. I wasn't amused either. I more pitied the child and his idiotic attempt to get a rise out of me by making such an insignificant challenge. The thought crossed my mind that I normally don't respond well to challenges, but this child wasn't deserving of significant pushback.

I put an apple slice in my mouth and bit down with a crunch. I stared at him for a moment while I contemplated his goal but decided that he was probably just a stupid child. Maybe he'd singled me out after listening to his mother constantly degrade his and his sister's fathers. The boy most likely had some kind of internalized resentment toward adult men after the conditioning he was subjected to. However, not my patient, not my problem. I was sure that some therapist could be frustrated at him in the future, but not me. I responded, "Good to know—lucky me," and walked back to the dining room table.

My toddlers had run off, most likely with their sister to play with the other children. Wonderful—now my only distraction had escaped, the moment I stepped away. I couldn't stand the idea of listening to the two adults jabber on forever, and I needed to find something that could absorb my focus. I looked at my wife. "Why don't we go outside? It's such a nice day."

The women agreed, and we all went outside while the children continued to play inside. I sat in an uncomfortable metal lawn chair at an ugly metal table that looked exactly like every other piece of cheap lawn furniture in the country. The wind was nice, and the birds provided something for me to watch. I contemplated if I was being rude by not participating in conversation but figured I was meeting the bare minimum standard of appeasing my wife and her desire to be social.

Part of me wanted to push through my discomfort and participate, but something about this woman seemed so toxic. Not toxic in the sense that most people mean when describing a manipulative or controlling friend. Toxic in a way similar to discarded biohazardous sludge that sickens or poisons everything. Every time her mouth opened, and sound escaped, it was a repulsive and disgusting statement.

She talked about both children's fathers, how worthless they were by walking out every time she would get mad and yell at them, and how horrible they were as fathers when they asked to meet halfway every other weekend instead of always having to drive to and from her house. She also complained that the one thousand dollars she received from each of them monthly didn't seem like a fair amount of child support when she had to deal with her kids 80 percent of the time.

It took everything in me to not vomit. I watched as

my wife also would occasionally seem uncomfortable with some of her statements, but I remembered what she'd said in the car about extending empathy because of what the woman had been through. I knew how compassionate my wife was, and she had a tendency to try to heal the birds with broken wings. It was a major difference between us, but I appreciated it in her.

Eventually I found myself needing to find a reprieve from listening to the conversation. I opted for an easy excuse, needing to use the bathroom, because no one pays much attention to time or asks questions when that's where a person is. I excused myself and walked back indoors, squeezing my wife's shoulder as I passed. She gave me a sweet and genuine smile. She could tell how miserable I was, but I think she appreciated my effort regardless.

I closed the sliding glass door behind me. I walked through the dining room, down the hallway, and into the bathroom. There, I stood in front of the sink and studied my face. Signs of irritation had built across it, the slightly furrowed brow and taut lips. I doubted anyone else would notice, but I needed to relax to prevent it from continuing to build. I stretched and rolled my neck to remove any tension that had nested itself in my muscles, and then I heard a familiar noise pierce the silence of the house.

It was crying.

I walked out of the bathroom and found the boy's bedroom door opened halfway. The crying was coming from inside. It wasn't the ear-shattering screams of a child in pain, instead a more muffled and whining cry, born from frustration. I harnessed the skills I normally only used to sneak into someone's home and peeked in. A spark ignited in my gut, and the flames began to spread.

My daughter was crouched in the far corner of the room. Her face was red, and fresh tears stained her skin. She looked up at the little girl that lived here, the previous target of her admiration, as the girl told my daughter that she was in time-out and wasn't allowed to talk or move.

A few feet from them, the portable crib was set up, and my twins were in it. The boy that had challenged me in the kitchen stood next to it and dangled toys above my twins' heads, just out of their reach. Their cries were what alerted me to the situation. They reached with all their might to get their toys, but the boy would jerk back before they could reach them.

I pushed the door open, and both of the minor residents of the house froze and stared at me. "What is going on here?" My voice was harsh and stern, but not like a father. It betrayed the predatory urges that I felt and the lack of restraint I could summon if I wanted to harm someone. Now, everyone in the room froze. The crying stopped, and all five children waited anxiously.

The adolescent boy looked at me. "We were just playing."

I walked to the cage my twins were in and lifted each of them out. They stood by my side, unmoving. I looked at the boy that was holding their possessions hostage. "Toys. Give them to me now." He did as commanded. I handed each child a toy and gave each a pat on the head. I didn't bend down or kneel next to them.

My body was incapable at that moment of making itself smaller for the sake of any of the room's occupants.

I looked at my daughter, who remained crouched in the corner. "Get up and come here." I tried to make my voice somewhat less aggressive as I addressed her. I didn't want her scared of me, but I didn't want her to question my directions. She stood up and moved past the girl that had towered above her before. I looked down at her. "Take your brother and sister into the bathroom. Clean up your faces, then go sit in the living room until I get there. Understood?"

She looked up at me. Her eyes were still red from her crying, but now they mostly looked innocent and confused. She took her siblings' hands in hers and led them out of the room. As they exited, I closed the door and turned to the remaining two children that were not mine. I took a couple of slow and intentional steps forward, stopping only one or two feet from them. I wanted them to feel trapped, like my children had felt. They joined each other and stood shoulder to shoulder.

The boy broke the tense silence first. "What are you going to do? You aren't our dad. You can't spank us."

I smirked. He had such a limited world view if the worst thing he could imagine was a spanking. I responded to him with a newfound calm in my voice that surprised me. "I can't? Are you sure? You seem to think it's okay to pick on people smaller than you. Why can't I do that?"

The girl began to respond. "We were just playing. We didn't think they would start crying. It isn't our fau—"

I interrupted her. "Shut it. You aren't allowed to speak." I felt that was necessary for how she spoke to my own child. "You were having fun harassing them. Making them cry. Scaring them. If that was so much fun, maybe I should try it." I took another small step forward.

The boy puffed his chest up and, I imagine, summoned every ounce of courage to look up at me and stand his ground. "Fine, go ahead. I don't care what you do."

My eyebrows rose. I was somewhat impressed by this defiance and bravery. I wanted to test him now. I knelt down and stared him in the eyes. "Is that so?" I looked at his hands as they clenched into fists by his side. "Those hands were being used to make my children cry, weren't they?" He stood still and resolute. I stared into his eyes with no emotion behind my own. "What if I broke those fingers so that you can never do it again. Would you care about that?"

I stared, watching as the moment he broke became obvious. He could either see or sense that I was being completely serious. The girl spoke up, her voice shaky and unsure, but it seemed she wanted to defend her brother. "If you touch us, I'll scream."

I turned to her. "You will? You'll scream like my children did? But your mommy didn't hear that, so why would she hear you? And then you have to hope she gets here fast enough." I turned my attention back to the boy. In my peripheral, I saw a dark spot start to form on his light-colored jeans.

I stood up and smiled at both of them. "Oh, come on. I'm just playing. Now, we can keep this a big secret, or you can tell your mom and see what happens if she decides to get angry with me." My smile never wavered as I turned and walked back out.

I went to my children in the living room to check on them. I explained that those other kids wouldn't bully them again and that it would only upset Mommy if she thought they had a bad time at her friend's house. My oldest, at least, understood what I was saying and agreed to keep it secret since I'd handled it. The other kids eventually came out, the boy in a fresh pair of pants, and the remaining half hour of our stay was calm and quiet. Their mother even made a comment about how calm her children seemed. We drove home and didn't speak about it again.

Maybe it was wrong to tell my children to keep secrets, but I needed them to. Somewhere between hearing that woman talk maliciously about everyone in her life and her own innocence, and watching that boy piss himself, something else broke in me. If I had built a prison for my darker self earlier in my life, then several experiences throughout that life had caused bars to become loose and fall off. This experience was different though. This experience had felt like the hinges on the prison door were completely blown off. My mind snapped seeing three of the four people I had grown attached to being threatened, and I was not going to let that be punished with light intimidation.

16

INNOCENCE

Innocence doesn't exist. People made it up with to make it easier to assign some amnesty to themselves or others they care about. To some, innocent describes an individual that has not done harm to others. However, this definition makes little to no sense, considering that a fetus's growth is physically traumatic to the mother as it incubates. We are all born having harmed another person.

It is almost unanimously agreed that children are innocent, but when is that innocence lost? When they become adults? When they have sex? When they have had enough neurological development to properly think through their own choices? Some people suffer traumatic brain injury and might have reduced capacity to evaluate their actions. Are those people now forever innocent?

From an external evaluator's perspective, it is easy to pass judgment. I doubt that many people turn that perspective back on themselves and ask, "When did I cease to be innocent?"

I have. I've considered if it was when I killed my neighbor, but I knew there was something dark even before that. I thought about the arson that accidently led to the death of two people, but that felt wrong in general. My own opinion is that I was never innocent. I was born into the world sullied and have only grown into it since then. And everyone else is the same.

No one is innocent. Sex, maturity, and actions don't alter you in any significant way. You were born a monster, just like me. The only difference is that I use my claws. And this isn't because some lady ate an apple a long time ago. It is because humans are corrupt, greedy, and violent creatures.

I used to imagine what my day in court would look like, and my first action would be to plead guilty. I know what I've done, and I don't care how that makes me look. After being caught, it would be insanity to try to pretend like I am innocent in front of people. Why is that so scary? Why do people fear being responsible for their own actions? People have a completely idiotic desire to be viewed as innocent in other people's eyes while they see themselves as the monster they know is in the mirror. What makes the appearance of innocence so important?

I know the appearance of innocence is important to me because it allows me to maintain freedom and relationships with the people I want. However, I hide things like murder. If I didn't hide that, I would go to prison and lose everything I've built. Other people hide stupid things to appear innocent, like sex or a previous addiction. Hiding those things does nothing for your life other than allow people to see you differently. It's a lot of effort for no actual benefit.

What irks me more than just people wanting to be innocent is the extent to which people will go in order to protect "innocence." Parents shielding their children from the world so they can remain "pure." What a crock. Everyone eventually sees how horrendous the world truly is, and only a small percentage become like me. We innately understand violence and selfishness. It is a part of who we are. Protecting people from human nature is akin to ice skating uphill; they are human, so it is their nature also.

Then, there are all of the ways to regain innocence. Don't worry, just because you did something that sullied you, just take these placebos and you can erase it all. The extent to which people find it necessary to dedicate time and energy to regaining something they never had is laughable. Forgiveness doesn't erase what happened. Catholic confession doesn't change human nature. Baptism is simply a cold dunk in water that does nothing to change whatever motives a person had for doing something wrong. If innocence can be restored, what is the purpose of going to great extents to protect it or passing judgment on those that lack it?

The number of people that don't think children are capable of great harm because they are too innocent is mind-boggling. Children are humans with the same base instincts as any other human. Protect your possessions, seek pleasure, and subjugate any that doesn't follow the pack. We are animals at the end of the day. Animals are capable of causing harm.

17

What I remember most about that night was the smell and feel of the musky air in the abandoned warehouse. It felt thick on my skin and made my breathing heavier. Sometimes I reflect on it and wonder if it was a physical response to the moral boundaries I had just crossed for the first time. I doubt it, though. The light from the small fire I had set for warmth and illumination showed the dust my steps kicked up. It was not the most sanitary of environments, but it served its purpose.

After leaving my wife's friend's house and witnessing my children being victimized by those bestial kids, the entire scenario stayed with me. I began looking for properties that were private and abandoned. This warehouse, or maybe it was an old slaughterhouse, eventually captured my attention. It was only thirty minutes or so from my house. There were still needles and trash littering the ground from the people that used the building to escape nature because they lacked another place to sleep. On this night, though, they had the money to get a hotel room if they wanted. I paid anyone I found a hundred dollars to stay gone for the night.

I recognized the risk then, and I'm thankful it didn't ruin me. Any of them could have ignored my offer and returned, or told others about what I was doing, but I think they were just happy to have the money. No one even asked me what I wanted the building for. A genuinely good group of people that minded their own business.

I set up shop in a basement area that was big enough for my needs. The floors were concrete, and the walls were all cinder blocks. Any lights or copper that had previously occupied the area had already been stripped away. I gathered some wood and made a small fire, and stood by it until I was ready to work.

It wasn't easy to get them to the building, down into the basement, and ratchet-strapped to the tables that had been left in the building. I managed, though. Sneaking into their house had been easy; I had become quite adept by this point.

They didn't fight or try to escape at any point. They knew they couldn't. I started in the young girl's bedroom. She was small and easy to control. I put a knife to her throat and a hand over her mouth to wake her. She quickly registered the danger she was in. I walked with her silently to her mother's room and used the threat of her daughter dying to control her. She helped me wake the boy and ensure his obedience. The intimidating black mask and the threats made it all too simple to get them to let me bind their wrists and mouth with duct tape.

I put them in the trunk of my car and drove to the location. I removed one person at a time, closed the lid, and performed a chokehold that ensured consciousness would give way within seconds. Then, I carried them through the warehouse and strapped them each to their own table. After one was secured, I returned to the vehicle and did it again to the next.

Then, I waited by the fire as each of them returned to their senses and desperately looked around the building, which felt more like a tomb than anything. I watched, curious what each would do. The children cried. The mother futilely attempted to yell through her duct tape gag. No one attempted to comfort the others.

I approached the mother, with no mask on, so that she could clearly see my face. Her eyes were confused and angry. I reached over and tore the tape off her mouth. "Don't scream. I don't have the patience to deal with it, and no one around here is going to hear you anyways." She consented by remaining quiet and staring me down, likely plotting how to hurt me.

"What the hell are you doing? I am going to tell your wife about this if you don't let us go right now." Her tone would have almost sounded confident and threatening if it didn't contain that trademark shakiness that clearly communicated fear.

"Actually, you would only be able to tell her if I let you out of here. You certainly can't tell her if you don't leave this place. Besides, do you really think I'm going to cave to some mundane threats at this point?" I turned away from her to the children, strapped to their tables. I expected to have mixed feelings about the image of two small humans bound and helpless. I had killed children before, but that was usually quick, over before they understood what was happening. I watched as tears filled their eyes and the blood left their faces. True terror.

The mother continued to speak to me even though I wasn't facing her. "Fine. What do you want from us?"

I turned, genuinely confused. This confusion happened often when I was preparing to kill someone. I expected the pleading and begging, or the defiant threats, but the inquiries and attempts to bargain always seemed odd. As if I'd planned the entire thing only to be dissuaded by some small side objective that they could fulfill. As I watched her and tried to determine how to respond to such a stupid question, she spoke again. "You aren't going to rape me, are you?"

I walked over to her and popped her on the forehead, like you would a dog who was attempting to steal food from your plate. It made a loud clap, and I leaned in. "Don't be gross. I have no interest in raping you, and it would be deplorable to bring your children along to watch. Besides, your mere presence and attitude disgusts me."

She seemed shocked and offended at my words. Another stupid response. She'd been tied up and thrown in the trunk of a car, but my disinterest in coitus with her was somehow offensive. She spat her question at me again: "Then what do you want from us?"

I took a deep breath to calm myself down.

Something about this woman set my nerve endings on fire. "Simply put, I want to kill each of you." Her eyes went wide in fear as I leaned in and hovered my face directly over hers. The children started to sob more loudly behind me. "You and your children are disgusting. It would be hard to describe you as anything more than human trash. You blame everyone else for all your problems. You have this entitlement that oozes from your every pore, and it infuriates me. Your children have already started to pick up on it. They're already half as vile as you." My tone never broke. I was giving her the education she desperately needed years before.

She mustered up some strength. "That's bold of you to say. You're going to kill three people, and you think we're the ones who are disgusting. Take a look at yourself."

"Oh, I have. I am absolutely every bit of the monster you think I am, maybe even worse. However, what I don't do is delude myself into thinking I am not." I paused. An idea came to my mind. This was a teachable moment. I stood tall over her again and moved to the side so she could see her children. "See, your little shit children thought it was funny to bully and harass people smaller than them. The boy there thinks it's a game to antagonize and push others to see how far he can take it. I have seen those behaviors before—in myself at his age. Actually, he might be a bit further ahead than I was. And your daughter, she is a piece of work. She lorded over my daughter and controlled her speech and ability to move. She took pleasure in removing another person's autonomy, much like the pleasure I took in gagging and restraining each of you. You are breeding two little monsters right now. So yes, I am going to hurt them. I am going to kill them. Because that is what monsters do, they devour other monsters. Tell me how you feel about that, Mommy."

I waited for her response.

She looked at her children as tears filled her eyes. I have never been the best at recognizing and differentiating between tears of sympathy, guilt, or fear. She looked back at me. "You're right. I don't know if it was me or their fathers, but I didn't know how to help them." Muffled screams and cries sounded from each of the children, unintelligible through the duct tape. The mother's words became more rushed and frantic. "I tried, honestly. We can do better now. After this, I'm sure they are going to want to change. Please, just let us go, and I will make sure that they get the help they need."

Her begging hung in the air like the scent of sweet dessert after dinner. Delectable. I savored every syllable as she failed the little test I'd chosen to give. My only response was to burst into laughter. I walked back toward her and put the tape back over her mouth. I gained control of my breathing as my laughter dissipated. "Wow, Mom, that was absolutely brilliant. In one moment, you managed to keep the blame on your children without actually taking responsibility for your role. You could've admitted fault, claimed they were innocent, and asked for them to be released. Instead, you agree with me and promise they'll get better? That little speech disturbed even me. You might look at me as the worst creature in the world, but I would gladly volunteer to accept all of the punishment if it meant sparing my children."

I walked away from her to the small duffel bag that I'd brought. I pulled from it a saw that I'd used to cut the same firewood that currently provided the only light in the room. I walked back to the middle, evenly distanced from each table. The light from behind my back danced and flickered, hopefully creating a very eerie effect with my silhouette. "Now, I have never done this part before, but I am going to explain what I am going to do to each of you so that you can fully understand the motive behind my actions. I normally wouldn't use something as old-fashioned or slow as this." I brandished the saw in the air, and the flexible metal made its signature sound over their weeping. "However, the cops have started to become suspicious of the recent killings, and I need to start changing things up. If I use different tools and methods, it should keep them off my trail for a bit longer. So, I do want to apologize for the archaic methods. I would prefer it to be fast, but what is good is also necessary."

I paused, allowing them a moment to accept my apology. Then I continued. "First, I am going to saw the little girl's legs off. Since she thinks she can look down on people, she should know what it is to be truly small. Then, I am going to saw off the hands of the boy, since he thought it was funny to use them to withhold joy from my children. And lastly, Mom, I am going to use this"—I pulled a small knife from my pocket—"to careful cut open your throat and pull your tongue through. Obviously, chances of survival for any of you are slim, but if anyone manages to survive, then you will be free to go."

I listened as each of them wrestled against their restraints and cried through their gags.

"Let's begin."

I sat on the dusty floor of the abandoned building. Sweat covered every inch of my body as I leaned back on my hands and looked at the ceiling. None of the three survived their treatment. When I started in on the mother, she barely moved as I started to carefully slice through tissue to open her throat. Her eyes were dull and lifeless; the shock of hearing her children's tortured cries had obviously broken her mentally. Once she had died, I went to work with the saw again and began carving the bodies into small pieces to make disposal easier.

Now, their body parts were all wrapped in the plastic wrap that I'd brought in my duffel bag. My clothes were already bundled and burned, and I'd changed into a fresh set that weren't completely covered in blood.

I looked down at my watch: 2:37 a.m. Still enough time to dispose of the pieces in the holes I had dug three days prior in some woods not far from the building. After that, I would get back to my hotel room and attend the second day of the conference that I'd told my wife I would be at. A smirk cracked on my face as I reveled in how well the plan was going to work. I'd checked in at the conference. Left. Got my bag together. Picked up my targets. Did my work. Now, I had a solid alibi, and even if the bodies did happen to be found, the modus operandi was so different from anything in the past that the police would never connect the dots.

I took a quick moment to reflect on the feeling I was experiencing. I had been expecting the sense of release that I had grown accustomed to with past victims, but this was different. It was elation. I truly enjoyed every part of it.

It was new, and it was nice. I thought about what was different. My eyes fell on the large duffel bag, and I realized that it was much more work than it had been in the past. That could lend itself to the increased pleasure and sense of accomplishment, but I knew that wasn't all of it. It was the act of relishing in the pain and fear of each of my victims. I had always focused on completing the task and moving on. Not this time. I watched as each member of that family lost all hope and accepted their fate before passing away.

I set out to finish my evening. By the time I returned home after the conference ended on the second day, I was still walking on clouds. I walked through the door and kissed my wife and greeted my children with large hugs. I felt amazing still. I'd originally experienced some concern that my feelings toward my family would be altered by that night. I had considered that it might shorten my fuse or result in me being more aggressive with them. However, no such negative consequence occurred. I knew that I had touched on a darkness within me that I would not be able to shut away again, but it didn't seem to encroach on my desire to keep these people in my life. My wife was excited when I walked in, and her bright smile was a welcome sight.

"What got into you? Did the conference go that well?" she asked, keeping her arms wrapped around my lower back.

I kissed her again. "Not really. It was decent for a psychiatry conference, but I am just overjoyed to be with my family again." A gave her a big smile and she nestled her head into my chest.

Technically, I didn't lie. The conference was average, or at least the part that I'd attended. I was happy to be home. If she had asked if something else happened over the weekend, I would have been forced to lie, but it is always nice to take solace in being able to provide honest answers because of closed-ended questions.

Time continued to pass as normal. I simply had a new task on my to-do list. I kept working, coming home to my children, and participating in social engagements with my wife. Yet I found my mind almost constantly drifting toward the idea of performing such an act again. I needed to temper my excitement in order to maintain my safety. I had made it this far by being careful about choosing victims and properly preparing for each murder. It was more difficult at this point, though. I wanted to feel it again. The divide between who I was and who I needed to be to exist in the world became much larger and harder to bridge.

I agreed with myself that I would wait no less than three months and no more than six between each act. If I waited too long, then my skills might diminish, or I might begin to feel strong urges to act impulsively.

Approximately four months after that night in the warehouse, I located my next victim. I already had chosen the location for my next act—a seemingly abandoned shed that hugged a river, probably for fishermen. I'd seen it while hiking the river with my wife one day when we were enjoying some time with just the two of us. She had made a comment about how creepy it looked, so isolated from sight until you got close to it. I dared her to enter it with me, using the guise of testing her courage and having fun, but truly wanting to survey the interior. It wasn't large; the only thing inside was a large wooden table, bolted to the floor. It would be perfect.

I was working late one night, and on my way home, a driver turned across three lanes of traffic because they were too impatient to wait for me, the sole other car on the road, and almost crashed right into me. The entitlement so blatant in their behavior sparked my anger. I followed them into a strip mall parking lot. The only business that was open was a liquor store. I scanned the area briefly and noticed that between the bars on the windows and the rundown conditions of the parking lot and sidewalks, this was unlikely to be a place with surveillance. I parked so that my car was blocked by his from the view of anyone in the liquor store and exited my vehicle.

A fairly large man got out of the car, saw me, and started to approach me with his chest puffed and arms cocked out some to make himself look bigger. It is amazing that humans think we are so much better than animals but still employ the same tactics against other members of the tribe challenging us. I made no attempt to appear like a threat, just walked up to him with no emotion. When he tried to get close enough to push his chest into me, I reached back and delivered a quick blow to the side of his throat, an effective method of disabling someone, because a fierce enough punch to the jugular interrupts enough air and blood flow to the brain to provide a second or two to finish the conflict.

After placing him in a choke long enough for him to go unconscious, I threw him in the trunk of my car. I searched his vehicle and found that the man had been drinking heavily already, as evidenced by the multiple empty bottles in the cab of his truck. I got back in the driver's seat and called my wife to notify her that the paperwork for insurance companies was taking longer than expected. I told her she should go to sleep without me, but I would wake her when I got home.

The kill went smoothly. I didn't have anything to secure the man to the table in the shed, but a broken knee can prohibit movement as much as any straps. I lectured him on common courtesy and how his entitlement risked the life of my children's father. After beating him for more than a short while with a tire iron, I littered his empty bottles throughout the shack and set fire to the dilapidated wooden structure. Police would eventually question if he had been there alone because of the extent of his injuries, but they'd find no evidence of any company. Fire clears away most things. The story would be that he and a friend had picked up alcohol from the store, then gotten into an intoxicated fight. While recovering from the fight, he somehow accidentally burned to death after injuring his leg. Police can only report on what evidence they have. I had used fire once before, long ago, but since the recent string of killings never involved it, they'd have no reason to suspect me.

The kill itself wasn't that important or significant, though. It was what occurred about a week after.

I returned home from work to find my wife sitting on the couch, looking more than a little upset. I weighed the pros and cons of the situation and decided it was the husbandly thing to ask her what was wrong. I sat next to her, placed a hand on her leg, and noticed how tense she was feeling. "What's wrong, honey?" I asked.

She didn't look at me, just kept looking down at her lap. "It's nothing. I'm just worried."

"Okay. Tell me what's going on. Maybe I can help." This was abnormal for her. The last time this happened, she was pregnant. My mind raced with hope that it wasn't the case again.

"Do you remember my friend?" she asked, and talked about our visit there a few a months ago.

I betrayed nothing on my face. "Yes. I remember her. What happened? Did you two get in a fight?" Inquiring about specific impossibilities is possibly the weakest form of manipulation, but it could be enough. I didn't often watch the news, but maybe some of her body had been found. I'd buried the different parts in four random places in the woods, randomly placing some in each "grave." Maybe an animal had dug something up, or maybe I hadn't been as thorough as I'd hoped.

She took a deep breath. "No, we didn't get in a fight. Actually, I haven't heard from her in months. At first, I thought she was mad at me and not taking my calls, but I tried to reach out to her at work and one of her coworkers said that she had been reported missing. She hasn't been home or anything. I'm really worried about her." Silence fell on us as she stared at my face. My mind worked overtime to decipher the best possible response. I needed to feign concern.

I wrinkled my brow and looked at her. "Oh...that's really weird. I don't know her that well. Is this like her at all?"

She seemed irritated. "What do you mean? No, it isn't like her to just disappear with her children. Who would do that?"

I was shocked. She rarely got angry at me, and it had never been in response to a question. She'd always known I'm not good at these conversations (even when I'm not being outright deceptive), but here she was, going on the attack. I scooted a few inches away from her on the couch and turned my body to face her more. "Well, I don't know. She seemed a bit impulsive. I didn't even know the kids were missing. I figured they were with their fathers. But if you don't want my opinion, I can just let you be."

Her face started to twist more with anger. "That's always your answer, isn't it? You ask questions, then you disappear. My friend is missing, and the best you can do is call her impulsive."

I felt iciness start to build up. This woman's tone was becoming a bit too aggressive for my liking. I didn't know what her problem was. I had put in the work to be a good husband, met her friends, helped with our children. I'd done everything she wanted, and at least to her knowledge, I had never had any indiscretion outside of our house. I felt my breath start to become shallower and the all-too-familiar tension grasp at my muscles.

"You want help? With a woman and her kids that are missing? What do you think I can do about it? I see women like her all the time with histrionic behaviors, who need to be the center of attention, shirk their responsibilities and keep their lives in upheaval. If you want some specific help, then ask for it. Do not get mad at me for trying to talk to you, when that is all you asked for." My voice was even and calm, but it carried an undertone of aggression. I knew I wouldn't harm her, but I did instinctively want her to feel intimidated. I wanted her to back off. I don't know if it was the tone she chose to use, or the topic she was addressing. Maybe I didn't want her to push too hard on a topic I was so directly involved with.

She stared me down, as if debating whether she should respond to my challenge with one of her own. Then she huffed and walked out of the room. I stood in silence, fuming to myself. I knew that if she kept pushing, there was a chance I would lose control. I didn't know what would happen if I ever lost control with her. My imagination began to postulate about what would happen if she or one of my children pushed me past my breaking point. It wasn't hard to picture them experiencing harm at my own hands, and that scared me. But that couldn't ever be reality, could it?

18

TRUTH

I have been told repeatedly in my life that people wanted the truth from me. My wife's friend wanted the truth about why I had chosen them, but the truth didn't make them feel better. My wife wanted the truth about what happened to her friend, but did she really? The police, the communities, and the world as a whole want the truth about my actions.

I would like it if truth could be nothing more than the objective and measurable facts of the world. The sky is blue. The Declaration of Independence was ratified in 1776. We have a plethora of evidence that supports these claims beyond any reasonable doubt. However, the world is much deeper than simple measurable data, sadly. When people discuss the truth about the world, it is usually situations that involve a significant amount of subjectivity. What is the truth about the quality of our society? What is the truth about equality between different groups of people? Ask ten different people these questions, and you'll get ten different answers.

The one aspect about truth I am convinced of is that it doesn't actually matter to the majority of people. They say they want the truth, but they claw and bite when it doesn't match their own worldview. They don't want the truth. They want *a* "truth" that makes them feel more comfortable or makes them feel special. They want the truth to be that they are special, even though there is no evidence to support that. So, in that sense, these people are not asking for the truth. They are asking for confirmation of a desire that they are uncertain of.

Deception is so wrong because the truth is so valuable. That mindset is laughable. What is valuable about the truth? The only value it has is if you change your mindset because of it, or it brings with it some inherent benefit. If scientists discovered that violence exists because people are greedy and self-centered, would anyone actually attempt to be more selfless? Not likely.

People also only seemed concerned about the truth when it is coming from another source. Their vehement demands for the truth don't stop them from lying. Patient after patient sat across from me in my office and lied because they had some personal motivation to do so. Then, the same patients would demand I be honest about my opinion of them. They didn't want the truth. They wanted to be told that they were liked so they could validate themselves.

In that sense, no one actually ever wants the truth. They want to be told comforting platitudes, because that is where the benefit is. There is no benefit in reality. The truth is that the world is a simmering cesspool, and most people wouldn't accept harm to protect another person. No one feels better knowing that. Knowing that out of eight billion people in the world, only three or four actually care about you is uncomfortable. Knowing that almost every relationship you ever have will end makes relationships seem pointless. But that's the truth.

19

The local news started running stories about the missing woman and her children. The children's fathers appeared in interviews, pleading for the return of their loved ones. The only thing more irritating than watching police officers and reporters discussing the details of one of my crimes was watching the same people plus community members speculate on what could have happened. It had been months. She was obviously not coming back. Accept the inevitable likelihood of her death and move on.

The tension between my wife and me didn't dissipate quickly. After the disappearance of her friend, she was on edge and paranoid. She watched the news closely and often spoke about getting a better security system for the house. I regretted my decision on occasion; I was always able to calm her worries when the victims on the television were distant and unfamiliar. Now that there was a connection with a missing person, it seemed she wouldn't ever calm. I did my best, but to no avail.

I proceeded with caution in our relationship after she first tried to talk to me about her friend being gone. I didn't want to tempt the fates by pushing her and seeing how far I would allow myself to be pushed back. I couldn't understand what finally caused her to stand up to me that aggressively. She had no evidence that I'd done anything to her friend. I assumed she finally realized that she needed more emotional support than I could ever offer. Either way, I recognized the danger my relationship was in.

Since I couldn't fix things, I resort to appeasing her. I didn't like the idea of cameras around my house, because they were able to track me as much as they tracked any potential threat. However, I eventually agreed. At times, she talked about moving, which I refused to do. This house was close to my work, close to the children's schools, and also convenient to many potential drop sites for bodies.

I stuck to my schedule. Every three to six months, I would find another target or targets. I had become a bit more daring in some of my acts by selecting larger groups. I once targeted an entire parent group because a year prior they had led the charge on banning multiple books from school libraries, solely because they didn't approve of the content. Restricting what others were exposed to because of personal bias left a sour taste in my mouth, and I kept the group's name in the back of my mind. It had seven members at the time that I felt it was appropriate to act—three couples and a single mother. It was shockingly easy to join a parent group, drug some snack foods, and wait for everyone to pass out. The trick to that one was that I couldn't move the bodies. I did miss out on some of the fun of tormenting my victims, but injecting air into their veins and watching them have heart attacks was still somewhat enjoyable. After that, I tampered with a space heater that ran on kerosene, leading the investigators to believe it was carbon monoxide poisoning.

Regardless, time moved on like the unstoppable juggernaut that it was.

It was maybe two or two and half years after my wife's friend went missing. I was sitting in my office completing paperwork one evening when I heard a knock on my door. I had no scheduled patients, so confusion was my first response. I closed my laptop and leaned back in my chair. "Come in. The door is unlocked."

The door creaked open, and standing in the hallway outside of my office were a man and woman dressed in cheap suits. I stood up and greeted my visitors. "Hello. How can I help you?"

They entered my office and stopped about halfway, where I met them.

The man extended his hand. He introduced himself and his female companion as two detectives with the police department. I shook both of their hands as the man introduced them. "We wanted to see if you had a few minutes to speak and maybe answer a couple of questions."

I felt my heart rate increase. I didn't need to feign my confusion looking at them, though. They could be here for any number of reasons, but the worst-case scenario was still definitely a possibility.

I stepped back and to the side and pointed to the two armchairs across from my desk. "Of course. Please, have a seat."

I walked back behind my desk and sat as well. I wanted there to be a physical boundary between them and me. If they decided to become more assertive or make a physical motion, moving around the desk would give me enough time to act if necessary. I folded my hands on top of my desk and looked at them both.

The male detective was somewhat older, with dark hair that was beginning to gray in spots. He seemed slightly out of shape, but not so much that he would be a pushover if this came to a physical altercation. His partner was a young woman with blond hair pulled tightly into a ponytail. She sat quietly and studied me. Her demeanor conveyed some sort of respectful subordination to her more senior partner, and it was clear that she was very new and very inexperienced.

They sat silently, waiting on me to make the first move. I had read tips like this about negotiations and whatnot, where the person who speaks first loses control of the conversation. Ridiculous. I spoke up. "So what can I help you with?"

He looked at me. "Well, we are sorry for interrupting you so late in the day. We weren't sure you would even be in your office." *Lie. If you didn't think I would be here, why would you show up?* "Actually, it's been a long day for us. Would it be too much of a bother to ask for some water or something?"

I smiled. I wasn't sure what he was trying to do, but it felt like he was trying to get me to let my guard down by making me more comfortable. "It isn't a bother at all. There's actually a small refrigerator over there." I pointed to the wall by the door. "I keep water in there for patients. Please, help yourself."

The female detective stood up and fetched two cold bottles. She handed one to her partner and held on to the other. Neither opened their bottle. *Interesting.*

The man spoke again, seemingly trying to appear as harmless as possible, as he looked around at the décor in my office. "This is a very nice space you have here. I can imagine the rent is pretty steep."

My impatience started to rise. I didn't like being treated like a naïve individual, and this was becoming pedantic. "Well, I merely rent from the building owner. As much as I would enjoy a conversation about real estate, Detective, I highly doubt that is what brought you two here. What is it that I can help you with?" This wasn't actual irritation; it was a calculated move to stop his prepared approach. I was already taken off balance by their presence—I wasn't going to allow them to use whatever strategy they had settled on before arriving.

The detectives looked at one another. The man spoke again. I began to question if the woman was mute or if she was some sort of bombshell designed to throw me off guard. She was attractive, but not enough to be considered distracting. I decided to ignore her completely to see what effect that would have on the conversation. "You're right. We didn't come to talk about your office. My apologies." Then they asked me if I was familiar with my wife's friend.

I cycled through possible reasons they were in my office asking about that woman. The explanation that required the least amount of assumptions was they discovered I had interacted with her at her house. Any other explanation would require assuming that they found body parts, that they'd connected me to the night they went missing, or there was a witness. Moving forward along Occam's razor would help me maintain my sense of calm for the time being. "Yes. She was friends with my wife."

He pulled a small notepad from the inside of his jacket. "Right. That's what we had heard. Did you ever have a chance to meet her?" His tone was even as he asked his questions while scanning the notepad.

"Yes. My family and I went to her house once to let the kids play together." I kept my answers clear and concise. Too much detail could seem defensive, and not enough could seem avoidant.

"No other time than that, though?" He looked up from his notepad and stared at me in the eyes.

I held my smirk back. Was he trying to catch me in a lie? "Not that I can recall. But that was a very long time ago, and I was meeting a lot of my wife's friends. I guess it is possible, but I can't say for certain."

He nodded and looked back at his notepad. "That makes sense. One of her other friends said you accompanied your wife to a barbeque at another person's house, and she was present for that."

"If you insist. As I said, it's difficult to remember."

He continued to nod and hum to himself. The irritation at his veiled confidence was beginning to get to me. My fear at their presence had all but subsided. However, I was too impatient to play this cat-and-mouse game. I wanted to feed that stupid notepad to the man and wash it down with the water he still hadn't drunk. "Right. That makes sense. Were you aware that she has been missing for quite some time?"

I paused and considered challenging the man to get to the damn point. I don't like long and drawn-out games of wit. However, I knew that becoming frustrated would not cast me in a positive light. "Yes. My wife informed me something like two years ago that she and her children went missing. She's been distraught about it since. I haven't stayed abreast of the case, though, if that's what you're asking."

He looked up again from his notepad. These choreographed movements of disconnection by looking away and then the sudden engagement might have been off-putting to someone else, but to me it was merely a waste of time. I was aware that when he looked away to draw me into a false sense of security, the female mute was still studying me, even if I didn't give her attention. "No, of course." He paused as if trying to grab a question out of the empty space between his ears before speaking again. "It is odd that you don't remember meeting her at the barbeque, but you can remember a conversation with your wife from two years ago."

That was it? That was his best attempt to stump me? I hoped he could do better than that. "Not really. I didn't know the woman during the barbeque, so her presence wasn't worth remembering. My wife's fear and sadness over her friend's disappearance is very much worth remembering. I actually had to upgrade my entire security system at home just so she would feel safe again. I had to install new deadbolts and window locks throughout the entire house." My answer was technically accurate and truthful.

He flipped the notepad closed but kept the page he was on marked with his finger. "Oh wow. That must have been a lot. You weren't scared though?"

I wanted to strangle him then and there for these stupid attempts to get me to break. This nice-cop schtick was annoying. "No, I wasn't. She either ran away with her children or she was abducted. I live in a nicer area than she did, so I wasn't worried about my family being abducted, and there's nothing to fear if she ran away. Either way, I trust the police to do their job."

The last part was a lie. If this was them doing their jobs, I was shocked that they found their socks every morning. I paused, thinking my answer was more than adequate, but then considered that this might be a good time to put him in the hot seat for a moment. "Should I be more concerned whenever someone goes missing?"

He would have to either admit that my lack of response to the missing woman was understandable and appropriate or admit that I should be more worried that him and his brothers in blue weren't doing their jobs.

He smiled at me. A thin and fake smile. Then the woman found her voice and spoke for the first time. "What was your opinion of your wife's friend?" I turned to face her. She was calm and confident. Her sudden interruption was either an attempt to throw me off or to rescue her partner. A woman asking me my opinion of an obviously unstable woman might be viewed as "thin ice." It was an interesting strategy—if they had thought that deep into it.

"Can you be more specific please?" I raised my eyebrows to signal my curiosity but also my impatience.

"What do you mean? I'm asking your opinion of someone. There's not really a specific question here." She seemed uncertain. Her question was genuine and uncalculated.

"Detective, you are currently sitting in my psychiatry office. I'm not sure if you're asking my opinion of her from a personal perspective or from a clinical one. What you're looking for specifically does change my answer." I didn't know what I was doing at this point. I think I was more playing with my food than desiring any specific outcome.

She thought about it for a moment. "Good point. I'd appreciate if you could offer both."

I took a deep breath. I had to walk a thin line at this point. However, if I did it well, it would provide greater evidence of my nonexistent innocence. "Well, my personal opinion is that she is a woman who went through quite a lot. She has conflict with both of her children's fathers. She is abrasive, which probably makes maintaining friendships difficult. When I visited her, she spoke at least twice as much as my wife, who is not a quiet person. However, the one, or possibly two, times that I interacted with her isn't a whole lot to get a great impression."

I paused to ensure I didn't want to add anything. "I am a bit more hesitant to share my clinical opinion. I never saw her in a clinical setting. So please understand that this is not official, and I can't share it with any degree of confidence. Would you still like to hear it?"

The female detective nodded for me to continue.

"She dressed somewhat provocatively when I remember meeting her, dominated the conversation, and needed for attention to be on her. These are surface-level signs of a condition called histrionic personality disorder. In simple terms, it is a person that wants to be the center of attention for everyone around them. If I am correct, these people can open themselves up to some significant risk. They will typically build very shallow relationships with others, but value them much more meaningfully than they actually are. Of course, that is based on one encounter that I can recall, so please take it with a grain of salt."

I stopped talking to give the detectives time to process what I had said. I know it was somewhat risky to plant the seed that maybe she ran off with someone, because trying to push blame off can give a bad impression, but it was framed through a professional lens, which would hopefully help. Technically, everything I'd said was accurate and truthful.

They both sat there and nodded along. The man jotted notes down as fast as he could while I spoke. Finally, the woman responded. "So, is it fair to say you didn't like her?"

I looked to the side and considered this. Such an odd question, and an odd way to phrase it. Whether or not I like someone has nothing to do with anything. "I wouldn't say that. She isn't my preferred company, but few people are. In my line of work, it's hard not to see someone for all of the mental health issues that they aren't addressing. It is very challenging to find people I would volunteer to spend a great deal of time with. She was simply a person with flaws, just like every other. I didn't really give a lot of thought to whether I 'liked' her or not."

They sat in silence again. They seemed unprepared for the answers I'd given. They kept looking at each other before turning their attention back to me as if trying to find a game plan for what came next. I decided to intervene before they were able to recover from absorbing such a massive amount of information.

"I don't mean to be rude, but I highly doubt that two detectives came to my office after 6 p.m. to ask me whether or not I liked a missing woman. I also don't think it's likely that you are going around to every single person she interacted with and asking their impressions of her, especially two years after the fact. I have answered your questions, so could you please tell me what brought you to my office?" I stared directly into the female detective's eyes as I spoke. She was more inexperienced. This level of direct challenging should cause her greater discomfort than the more veteran crime fighter.

The man spoke up again, apparently finding his bearings. "You aren't wrong, sir. We aren't going to everyone, just to you. I think we would be happy to share our reasons if you would be willing to come down to the station with us and answer a few more questions."

He'd played his hand too early. He wanted me to go with him to give him the environmental advantage. However, I was not curious enough or intimidated enough to relinquish that much control. "No thank you." I stared at him blankly, waiting on him to make his next move. I didn't want to give an explanation at first; I didn't want to give him any avenue to approach getting his desire met.

He sat stunned and staring at me for a moment, then chuckled. "Well, I don't know if you have much of an option, sir." His voice was heavy with condescension and sarcasm. It seemed like I had rattled him at some point in the conversation. "We have some more questions for you, and it would be best if you came with us to answer them. You can try to refuse, but we could just arrest you and take you if you would prefer."

I looked over to his female partner, who seemed incredibly uncomfortable with what was transpiring. "If that's what you would like to do, then be my guest. If you truly thought that I did whatever it is you want to question me on, you would have shown up with an arrest warrant. So, you are either uncertain, or you have no grounds to arrest me. I have entertained every question you have posed, and I am sorry if they weren't the questions you wanted to ask. I would be more than happy to continue this conversation right here if you would like, but only if you cut the games and are more straightforward with me. If you choose to arrest me, I will gladly exercise my right to remain silent and not speak another syllable. What would you like to do, Detective?"

I knew this wasn't the smartest way to respond. Making an enemy of the police was never in my plan. However, I couldn't allow them to fully control the situation. I had to put them into a reactive mode so that I could take some power. I offered to continue talking because it demonstrated my willingness to cooperate. I didn't argue with his right to arrest me if he wanted. The line felt thinner under my feet with every step.

The tension hung in the room, heavy, until it was crudely cut by the female detective. "We received an anonymous tip that you might have had something to do with her disappearance." Her words were hasty and pressured. Her partner shot her a shocked look. She'd revealed their cards before he was willing to. This was good news, though. Her revelation showed that even she recognized they had very little to go on. A tip is easy enough to obscure and invalidate.

I sat back in my chair. "Okay. That's odd. Seeing as how I only met her twice apparently, I don't know why I would have any justified reason to have conflict with her."

The man closed his notepad and leaned forward. He put his weight on his elbows as they rested on his knees and gave me a smug look. "I have a little theory about that. You said yourself that she was dressed provocatively. Maybe you and her had a little tryst and you wanted to hide it. I don't know if you hurt her or paid her to go or what, but I'm not so inclined to turn down a tip when it comes."

"You put your faith in an anonymous tip? I think it is commendable to trust the public to such an extent, but what was so significant about this tip that you decided to visit me?" I wanted to push a bit further to see if they were holding out on me.

He smiled ear to ear and showed off his coffee-stained teeth. "Nothing. But a tip about a case that isn't getting any media coverage tends to be genuine, in my professional opinion." He placed emphasis on those last two words.

I wondered if he was bothered enough by my clinical status that it was causing some insecurity. "Fair enough. Decent point. So go ahead and ask me the real questions, and let's get past this."

The woman took over again, most likely sensing the undercurrent of back-and-forth between her partner and me. "She was last seen on June 23. That was a Friday. Where were you around the time she went missing?"

I furrowed my brow. I was thinking, just not about their question. I already had my alibi and my plan made up. I was thinking how long was appropriate to consider the question before searching through my calendar. I counted out ten seconds in my head, then responded. "I can't remember that long ago. Let me take a look to see if I have anything in my calendar from that time." I removed my keys from my pocket and turned around to my personal filing cabinet. I opened it and shuffled through its contents until I found my planner from two years prior. I placed it on my desk and started to turn through the pages.

As I searched for June, the male detective spoke again. "You just keep old calendars locked up in your office? That's kind of odd, isn't it?" His smug voice would have bothered me more if I didn't already have easy enough answers to disprove every stupid theory he tried to suggest.

"Not in my line of work." I continued to scan the pages for the day in question. "I have to keep client records for several years. Technically, that doesn't include my calendar, but in case there's ever a note I jotted down in my calendar about an appointment, I keep them for just as long. Lucky us." I looked at him and gave him a quick smile. It was innocent enough but conveyed every ounce of my challenge to try again. "Ah. Here it is. June 23. I was at an APA conference that weekend. I drove down on Friday night, got set up in my hotel room, attended the nine hours of lectures the next two days, and returned on Sunday evening."

The detectives looked at each other to consider the best response. The woman spoke first. "Would there be anyone who could corroborate this information?" The man looked disappointed. He saw his flimsy theory slipping through his fingers.

"Well, my wife can probably attest to me being gone. There were somewhere close to two hundred other clinicians at the conference, so I'm sure one or two might remember me being there. Of course, that was two years ago, so I can't say for certain. I would be happy to give you the board's information so you can try and get the list of attendees to question them if you would like." My voice was calm and measured. I didn't care if they questioned anyone. I went to these conferences all the time, and memory is fickle. If they questioned anyone I regularly interacted with, they would probably say I was present through assumption just based on my regular attendance.

They shared a glance again. She spoke for them both. "I don't think that would be necessary. Do you know of anyone who might want to harm her?"

This was an odd question. It went from so directed at me and my opinions to an actual fact-finding inquiry. "I can't say I do. I only remember meeting her the one time. As a mandated reporter, if she had revealed to me that she thought she was in danger, I would have had to report it to the police." The temptation to point her in the direction of her children's fathers was beyond tempting. However, I knew that was playing with fire. Besides, with how willingly she spoke about those relationships with everyone, I was sure that the idea had already occurred to them.

The male detective shoved his notepad back into his cheap jacket pocket as he spoke. "Well, thank you very much sir. This was a thin lead to begin with, but we appreciate your cooperation. We are sorry for taking up your time." They both started to stand.

I stood as well, showing my good manners. "It was not a problem. If you have any more questions, you are welcome to come see me." They started to turn to walk out the door. The man's shoulders hung heavy with disappointment and defeat. I stopped them before they moved away from their chairs. "Please don't forget your water. I don't want you to be too thirsty on your ride back to the station." They collected their unopened bottles and exited my office.

My body relaxed. I didn't realize how much tension I had experienced during the conversation. I wasn't worried about the police or their infinitely idiotic theory that I killed her to hide an affair. That was insane, and there was no proof of it. Let them chase their tails as much as they wanted. I was more concerned with this anonymous individual who thought it necessary to point them in my direction. Some coward who thought they had a theory but wasn't confident enough to give their name.

It couldn't have been the homeless people from the warehouse. They wouldn't have been reliable enough to trust, and they wouldn't know enough about me to get the police this far. The bitch's neighbors were out of the question. They would have provided any information they had much sooner than now. The fact the detective stated he thought I might have relocated her meant their body parts were still yet undiscovered. I rolled through my memory like a film in fast-forward. No witnesses. No interactions with anyone that knew me. No survivors for certain. I sat in my office for more than thirty minutes, analyzing that night over and over again. I tried to find the one weak link that might be the cause of my downfall.

Then it hit me. It was obvious. Painfully obvious. I gritted my teeth at my own ineptitude. I didn't know if it didn't occur to me immediately because the connection was thin, or because I wanted it to be less likely. However, once I started thinking why a person would provide the information but not their name, the answer became clear.

It was my wife. She had been so tense about everything. She had been suspicious of my lack of compassion for her friend's disappearance. She even knew before I met the woman that I wouldn't like her. I had made the assumption that her constant and consistent concern in the house was about external threats. Yet these two years had seen a marked decrease in our bond. It must have been because she suspected me the whole time.

It made sense. I was attracted to her initially because she was smart and could read people well. She would most likely refuse to give her name so that the police wouldn't identify her. This ensured her safety if she was correct and provided security that the police wouldn't show up at our house to question her making the report if she was wrong.

I sat stunned. I'd expected that I would eventually be brought down, but I'd never expected it to be a result of betrayal. I loved her and did everything that I could to protect her. The realization became all the more possible as I also remembered that she was letting our children stay with her parents for a week this week. I concluded that the seemingly innocent decision was most likely to protect them in case I was arrested. She had planned to betray me, and now she was at home by herself, waiting to see the results of her action.

I stood up, gathered my belongings, and began the drive home.

20

DEATH

The Rider-Waite tarot deck has a card in it that signifies death. The card doesn't actually represent the end of a person's life but instead a major change that is coming. Yet conversationally, when we discuss death, it is almost unanimously about a person whose existence has expired. Comparing these two different definitions of death, I have never understood why the life-ending definition has intimidated people more. Life is supposed to end. Change can be scary because there is a degree of uncertainty about what new challenges will present themselves. However, there are no future challenges after you physically die.

What is scary about life ending? I am not religious. I do not believe in an afterlife. I do not think that there is any world outside of the one I currently exist in. You live and then you stop living. I don't find this scary. A painful death might be scary because pain is scary. However, no longer existing has always been a comfort to me.

People fear death because each of them wants to think they are somehow unique. They don't want to say that they are the same as every other person they meet. They avoid the idea of dying because, in their minds, the world would somehow be irreparably changed by their absence. They can avoid the cold grasp of the reaper somehow if they can avoid the topic altogether. God will allow them to live for eternity if they somehow do not invite the Pale Rider into their lives by uttering his name or accepting he is inevitable.

I fear death for only one reason. I would no longer be able to protect what is mine. My children would have to rely on others for safety and proper education about the world. I could die more comfortably if I trusted that those children would be guaranteed a meaningful life, but I do not trust that other people can mold them to pursue that. I didn't even trust their mother enough to feel confident that she would guide them in the direction I thought was important. I had to accept that my legacy, my children, are in the hands of others in order to be more comfortable with my death.

Death is inevitable. Legacy is uncontrollable. Change is inescapable. Regardless of how you view death, fighting it is a waste. For each and every one of us.

21

I drove home from my office in somber silence. I sometimes would play music to provide some stimulus other than the moronic drivers littering the streets. However, on this day, I was not in the mood for music. I kept playing what I suspected to be true in my head. *My wife called the police on me. She is trying to take everything that I have worked for.*

I couldn't be certain; I had no direct and tangible evidence. I couldn't very well tell the police that they had no proof and then act exactly like them. But this was the only option that made any sense. She knew I was gone that weekend. She knew I didn't like the woman. She knew I didn't respond to news of her disappearance. She knew me better than anyone, and if there was no direct witness to the act itself, the person who knew me best might suspect me most. All of this made sense.

I pulled into my driveway and sat for a second. It had been a while since I had taken a thorough personal inventory of my state without considering the perception of another. I felt like a child again, learning to look at myself and assess my state. I noticed that I didn't feel anything. I wasn't experiencing the typical heat of rage or the iciness of my cold and calculated anger. There was no tension in my muscles, no elevation to my biorhythm. I was in a state of perfect calm.

I was about to confront my wife, who might accuse me of being the murderer that I am. My emotional ineptitude had always been a comfortable blanket that shielded me from the depth of pointless experiences that other people wrestled with. However, I found myself wishing I felt more in that moment.

I considered if I should create a plan. Try to devise a method of confronting her and discovering what she knew and what role she'd played. However, as I started to shuffle through the possible approaches I could take, I found myself running headfirst into a brick wall. There was only one outcome that seemed to carry further into the future beyond this night. If I was completely wrong and she had no suspicion, then we could continue living like normal. If that was not the case, then everything I had become accustomed to was about to be stripped away.

Each avenue I considered led to the same dead end. A mental image of my children. My children. They were mine. I would never have said I was extremely close with them, but the thought that this night could dictate if I ever saw them again was a dark cloud hanging over me.

I climbed out of my car and into the light from the

streetlamps. I walked toward my door, keeping to the walkway and not dirtying my shoes in the grass. I punched the code for the front lock and opened it.

The house was dimly lit, with only the lamps in the dining room providing illumination. I saw the silhouette of the woman I once chose to let into my life sitting on the sofa with her head in her hands. As she heard the door close behind me, her head shot up in my direction. The lighting wasn't bright enough for me to see her specific expression. I placed my bags down and flipped a switch to turn on the rail light that I had hung in the living room.

With the brighter light, I could see her face more clearly. Skin flushed. Eyes puffy and red. Expression wide in shock. She was crying and seemed surprised to see me. She stood up, wiped her face, then dried her hands on her jeans. "Honey, I didn't hear you come in. It's late. What kept you so long?" Each word was shaky and weak.

I removed my jacket and hung it on a hook by the front door, then loosened my tie so that it hung flaccid around my neck. "Yes, sorry I didn't call. I had a very odd evening. But what about you? You look like you've been crying." My words had no emotion to them. It would have been easy for any listener to discern the coldness behind the inquiry.

She stayed standing in the living room, and I stayed near the front door. It felt like a standoff. The distance between the front door and that couch was an infinite expanse that would close quickly once one of us stepped forward. "Oh, yeah. I've been crying a bit. But it isn't a big deal. I'd rather hear about your day."

My eyes narrowed. This response wasn't completely uncommon for her, so it didn't lend itself to me discovering anything new. "Nonsense. Sit at the bar and I'll make us both some tea. Apparently, we've both had less than optimal days. We can talk while I get the water boiling."

She gave me a small smile that seemed more like a mask than any genuine appreciation. "Okay. That sounds nice. Let me go to the bathroom and clean up first." She walked out of the living room, down the hall, and into the bathroom.

I moved into the kitchen, turned on the overhead lighting, and filled the teapot with water from the sink. The silence was uncomfortable. I felt each of my nerves on full guard, waiting for some kind of attack. I placed the teapot on the stove and started to fill up two teabags with some green tea I had ordered from Japan. I then stood in the kitchen, leaned against the counter with my arms crossed, and stared past the bar and into the hallway she would emerge from. I knew my demeanor and expression weren't inviting, but I couldn't bring myself to show any sign of vulnerability.

Eventually she emerged and took a seat on one of the stools at the bar. She looked at me and smiled. Her face was still flushed, but she had tried to erase the signs of her previous weeping. There was a moment of silence before she spoke. "So do you want to tell me about your day first?"

I cocked my head to the side. "No, I'm worried about you. I thought you'd be enjoying your day while you had a break from the children. What's going on?"

Her eyes moved side to side for just over a second while she searched for an answer. She was either nervous to tell me or she was forming a lie. "Yeah...I think I'm just feeling kind of hormonal. I was thinking about how much older the children are getting and how much has changed. I think that just made me kind of sad."

That wasn't bad. Blaming hormones was a good tactic. It allowed her to skirt the question while providing some justification for her mood. Instead of stating some obvious reason to cry, she fell back on making herself look foolish and irrational. I was reminded, at that moment, why I married her. "Well, that makes sense. Fear of change and our children no longer being babies any more can be tough. A lot of parents get sad as they realize that one day they won't be needed as much."

She sat there and studied me as I answered. Her eyes narrowed as she absorbed my words. Her left hand shook slightly as I was talking, betraying her nervousness. "Do you ever get sad thinking about it?"

I looked away. That was a perfectly reasonable question, but also a question heavy with subtext if she suspected me of something sinister. "Of course I do. Not to the point of tears though. I think I'm more excited to see what they grow up and become. I want to be there for them to ensure that they can be happy later." A question designed to see her response about my future in the family. She simply nodded.

The teapot started to scream, and she jumped at the sudden interruption. I turned my back and grabbed two mugs from the mug tree. I placed them down, filled them with steaming water, and then dropped a teabag in each. I turned around to hand her one of the mugs and smiled. "Are you okay? You seem jumpy."

She chuckled. "Yeah. Just came out of nowhere." She paused. "What happened to you today? Tough sessions?"

I took a sip from my tea, allowing more silence to enter the conversation. I wanted to measure her discomfort and how it changed throughout the conversation. Her shaking hand and the sudden perspiration on her forehead signaled to me that she was getting more nervous. "No. All my patients went really well, actually."

"That's good, then." She took a sip of her tea.

"It was after work that got odd. I had two detectives come to my office and visit me." I stopped there to study her reaction. Her eyes went somewhat wide, but her mouth stayed unmoving. I had learned that this was typical for her when she was faking an emotional response. She didn't seem capable of displaying an emotion with her full face when it wasn't genuine.

"Oh no. What did they want?" Faux concern. A half-assed mask to keep the conversation going. I realized that she was gauging my reactions as much as I was hers. She took another sip of her tea and for the briefest moment averted her eyes.

I knew then that my suspicions were correct. She wasn't genuinely shocked about their visit, and there was no actual concern about the myriad possible reasons they could've been there for. She was already aware of all this information—or at least aware that there had been a possibility.

"They actually wanted to ask me a bunch of

questions about your friend that went missing. I thought that was particularly odd, considering how long it's been." I stood staring at her. I knew this woman. I knew she was smart enough to know that I was already suspecting that she was the cause. If she wasn't, then she had fooled me for a very long time and was actually much dumber than I gave her credit for.

She gave me a confused look. "That is weird. What did they ask you?" She kept nervously sipping at her tea.

"At first, they just wanted to ask me about how many times I met her, what my experiences with her were like, and then they asked about my clinical opinion of her. It seemed like they were convinced I'd met her more times than I had. One of them even brought up a barbeque that they said she was at. I didn't really remember that."

She let out a weak and forced chuckle. "Well, you never were good in groups of people. I'm glad the police are still looking for her, though. That's kind of reassuring right?"

She started to stand up as if the conversation were over with that final question. As she turned away from the bar, I spoke again. "That's not all."

She froze and turned to look at me with an expression of surprise. "Oh?"

I placed my teacup down and moved toward the bar so that only that slab of marble separated us. "Apparently, they received an anonymous call. The person accused me of having something to do with her disappearance. I'm not sure if that person told them about the barbeque or what, but the police were under the impression that I was involved with her going missing."

Her response was a pitiful laugh followed by, "That's crazy. Who would think that?"

I walked around the bar and sat in the stool next to her, facing away from the countertop. I felt her body tense as I sat directly beside her. I was hoping that she would slip more and make a comment that easily allowed the accusation to be made, but she played the game cool and calm. She gave short, concise, and direct answers. We were almost a perfect match. Almost.

I sighed. I didn't turn to her as I spoke. "Stop. I don't feel like doing this anymore. I just want to know why you would do it."

My words must have hit her like anvils. The silence was deafening. It felt like the entire world stopped turning for a moment. She knew that she was caught, and now I had to wait on how she reacted. She turned on the stool to face me, and I felt how harshly she had to brace her body to do so. "What are you talking about? What do you think I did?" Her words came out through held breath, each syllable shakier than I'm sure she intended.

I reached up and rubbed the corners of my eyes. I felt an irritation start to build. I could respect how she'd handled the conversation up this point. She had earned greater leeway than anyone else in my past. However, talking to me like I was stupid after being confronted directly was an affront to my intelligence. It was also beneath her. "I'm not kidding. Stop playing ignorant. Tell me why."

The tension released from her body, and her shoulders began to sag. She had given up the charade. Good. I wasn't going to last if she persisted.

She stood up and moved in front of me. Apparently, she had found some courage with the dropping of her deception and wanted to confront me face-to-face now. "I don't know. I called because I've had this gut feeling for too long now. I knew something was off when I told you about her being missing. I replayed that conversation in my head so many times since that day, and I finally figured it out. You asked me questions to try and learn more. You didn't show concern or sympathy or anything really. You were curious. I knew something was off then."

I stayed seated and looked at her. From my position on the bar stool, and her standing in front of me, our eyes were at the same level. I looked into them and saw the hurt, the betrayal, the anger. I didn't see fear, though. She suspected I had something to do with it, but it didn't seem like she suspected what had actually happened. "Okay. Understandable. You became concerned because I wasn't sympathetic. But you called the police. Why didn't you come and ask me about it?"

She crossed her arms, taking the dominant position. She seemed invigorated, prepared to justify her actions. "Well, you said you don't remember the barbeque, but I do. You and she talked for something like thirty minutes that day. I saw that she was flirting with you, and you didn't stop her. So, what was I supposed to do? Accuse you of cheating and then paying for your little girlfriend to leave? You would call me crazy and somehow use some twisted logic to prove me wrong. So, I told the police, hoping that they could figure it out and find her. Then you couldn't deny it." Her words were as accusatory as they were certain and aggressive. Her face was stern and unrelenting.

It was all the more surprising to her when my only response was uproarious laughter. It wasn't the type of laughter elicited by some passing joke. I felt this come from my gut. She became all the more defensive in response. "Don't laugh. I know that you've been withdrawing money and putting it somewhere for a long time now."

I waved my hand at her to try to get her to stop as my laughter subsided. I took a few deep breaths to regain my composure. "No, you're right. I have been taking money out of the account. But I definitely wasn't giving it to some mistress hidden away somewhere."

She became more agitated. "Okay, smart guy. What are you doing with it, then? I'm not an idiot. I know you don't gamble. I know you don't do drugs. I thought that maybe you had some kind of addiction since you stay out late sometimes, but you don't show any other signs. So if it isn't an affair, what is it?"

I smiled at her. It was a genuine smile. She had watched me, gathered evidence, and come to the conclusion that seemed most rational. This was the woman I loved. Certainly, she came to the wrong conclusion, but I felt the desire to be honest with her about the money. She had done so much work; she deserved some honesty from me for once. "I hide it. I pull out two thousand dollars in cash each month and store it in a PO box in case I ever need to leave and need funds to survive."

She rolled her eyes and kept her arms folded across

her chest. "Do you think I'm an idiot? Why would you need to have some sort of 'go-bag' of cash? Are you going to try and convince me that you're a spy who might put us in danger one day?"

I continued to smile at her. I have never subscribed to the idea that a person can see their life flash before their eyes, but that is the most accurate description for what I experienced. I saw her as the waitress serving me my food. I saw her on our first date. Our wedding day. The birth of our children. Memories that for any other person would be so cherished that they would never allow them to slip into obscurity. I had, though. This might have been the first moment I experienced some type of nostalgic response. Already middle-aged and still having new experiences, and only because of this woman. She was something special.

"No. I'm not a spy." I paused and noticed a shift in myself. I wasn't sure what changed for me in that moment. Maybe it was relief that my wife trusted me enough to not suspect me of murder. Maybe it was the respect I had for her observational skills, and feeling more connected to her through that. Regardless, I felt light, and I didn't want to keep having to hide myself. I continued. "I'm a serial killer."

Initially, she rolled her eyes. The idea must have been too farfetched for her to accept at first. But then, her face went lax. Her eyes darted back and forth as she started to replay other moments from our relationship. Every news report she had watched. Every night I came home late. Every time that she saw glimpses of my rage bubble to the surface. They must have played like a movie in her mind. The look of horror that crept onto her face showed that she eventually believed me, and the betrayal she felt was a deeper wound than any affair could have caused.

I, on the other hand, felt a sense of relief. I had never been this open and vulnerable with her. In fact, I don't know if I had ever even said those words so directly to any victim before. There was peace in finally speaking it.

When she started to turn on the ball of her foot to make a run for it, I was ready. I pounced forward and grabbed her by the wrist. She was much smaller and weaker than me, so it was easy to pull her back to me. We stood next to the kitchen bar as she turned back and slapped me in the face. It stung, but she deserved to do that much at least.

I gripped tighter. "Stop. Please don't run. I don't want to chase you."

Tears started streaming down her cheeks as she kept swinging her hand at me. I used my grip on her wrist to turn her body and wrapped my other arm around her throat. I had done this move to enough people; it was second nature at this point. I applied enough pressure to the sides of her neck to impress my seriousness on her. Her movements calmed, but she did not.

"Get your fucking hands off me, you monster." She pushed the words through gritted teeth. I wish I could say that her words hurt, but she wasn't wrong. I was a monster. I think the only part that bothered me was realizing how little she actually knew about me.

I was tired of the façade. I felt her warm tears fall

onto my arm as I squeezed. It would take mere seconds for her to go unconscious once I applied enough pressure to the choke hold.

I spoke to her in a whisper. "Shhh. Calm down. I'm just trying to talk to you."

She wrestled against my arm, but it was getting her nowhere. Her fight was dying down as the grief began to consume her. Her weeping grew stronger as her strength diminished. "Screw you. I don't want to hear what you have to say. If you're going to kill me, then just do it. But you better never lay a hand on my kids."

My first thought was how pointless that statement was. She was volunteering to die while threatening me in the same breath. However, that thought vanished very quickly. I felt hurt. Genuinely hurt. I couldn't fathom what would make her consider that I would do such a thing. "Do you really think I would hurt our children? I have done everything for you and those kids." My voice was less of a whisper now. It was agitated at her accusation. I didn't understand how her brain was even capable of forming such a thought.

My arm stayed around her neck, but her fight was gone. Her body rested against mine. Both of her hands lightly grasped the arm that could easily rob her of oxygen, but she didn't try to pull it away. It felt something like an embrace between two lovers, but I knew there was no affection from her now. She took a few breaths to calm her crying. "How many people?"

"I don't think that's really important. You aren't going to feel better knowing that." I wanted to answer her questions, but I didn't feel safe enough to place every sordid detail on the table to be analyzed.

She paused and considered my answer. Her voice was weak and filled with the sadness of the betrayal she was feeling. "Fine. You don't have to tell me. Just answer one thing...why?"

She had one reasonable request, and I felt a pit grow in my stomach, because it was the one thing I didn't know if I could answer. I had contemplated that question so much in my past that I had quit trying to find the answer. I felt like responding with "I don't know" or anything resembling it would be unfair to her. Her life was dissolving just as quickly as mine.

"I can't give you an easy answer to that. I think it's always been a part of me. I tried to control it but eventually couldn't do it anymore."

Her voice responded with a resurgence of some of the previous irritation. "I don't believe that. I've known you for so long. I've seen you be a good person. And now you're saying that was a lie?"

Instinctively, my arm squeezed tighter when I heard her irritation. I felt her body start to tense, and I realized what I was doing. I relaxed some. "It wasn't a lie. I really did everything I could to be the best man possible for you and those kids. That's why I hid all of this from you. I don't want this to tear our family apart."

"You did everything? You could have not done any of that in the first place. You could have tried to get help. You had options. Instead, you chose to lie and hide all of it. Our whole life together was a lie, and no matter what, you are never going to see those kids again."

That was when I felt it. The ice poured into my veins and spread throughout my body. I went cold, and my arm started to squeeze harder around her neck. "It wasn't a lie. I cared for you, and you betrayed me. I did everything to protect you, and them. Yet you think you can threaten me and keep my children away from me? You are in shock right now. You should calm down before you push this further than it needs to go." I know she heard it in my voice this time. Actually, I know she had heard it before, but this time she recognized what that tone, devoid of any emotion, meant.

She froze. Her intermittent sniffles represented the end of her crying. She spoke again, this time somewhat hoarse as the words had to push past the force inflicted by the pincer of my forearm and bicep. "That doesn't matter. Maybe you have been there up till now, but what happens next? How long can you hide all of this from them? What are you going to do if they ever find out?" She paused and tried to suck down a few deep breaths to allow her to finish. "You and I are over. If this is who you are, then you aren't who I thought. And I hope you can admit that our kids will never actually be truly safe with you."

As those last words left her mouth, I moved on reflex. My arm squeezed tighter, and after a couple seconds of gurgling, her body went limp.

22

After she fell unconscious from the choke, I laid her body down on our floor. I stood over her for what might have been a minute or might have been an hour. I couldn't tell. Time froze for me. Her body lay strewn at my feet, helpless.

I thought about the fact that my life could have continued if I finished the job. If I did the one thing that I excelled at above all others, I could move forward like normal. I also knew that was a complete lie that I was trying to tell myself. Nothing would be the same again. She had been the cornerstone of this life I built, and without her, it would all crumble.

The truth was what she had said. Those children would have no meaningful future with me around. They would eventually start to notice my absence throughout the weeks, or they would develop the same shallow emotional range that was the extent of my capabilities. They would eventually become more curious and start asking questions. When I couldn't provide them with sufficient answers, they would start trying to figure it out themselves. What would I do then? I would never be able to fully trust teenagers with that knowledge, and it would lead to the most obvious outcome.

Without her, they would be getting a one-sided approach to life. It was the same side that led me to standing above my wife contemplating if murdering her would be the easiest route. I imagined their futures with no meaningful connections, and it filled me with enough despair to know that it would be wrong to let my presence be the leash that held them back.

The truth was harsh, but I knew I couldn't fight it. I quickly pulled an envelope from the counter and found a pen. My mind raced with what I would write, but I decided she deserved some form of closure.

I won't be so disrespectful as to offer you excuses. I hope you know that I am grateful for the years I spent with you. I hid a lot of myself, but I know that you were the one that brought out the best in me. Take care.

I got in my car, and I left. I didn't grab any personal items or family memorabilia from the house. I drove to the PO box that I had kept secret for so long and pulled the hefty black duffel bag from inside. I carried it out to my car, placed it in the passenger seat, and opened it to check its contents. A very large sum of cash that had grown each month for years, and a picture of my wife and three children. I changed this picture only once every six months or so to keep up with the children's growth. I never understood why I did this ritual until I was sitting in my car right then, staring at it.

It wasn't that I wanted to remember them. I wanted it to remind myself of the closest I ever came to being human.

I drove to the nearest airport, left the keys of the car in the wheel well, and bought a ticket to Thailand. I had done my research and figured it would be the easiest location to change my identity and disappear. I figured that it was far enough away from the consequences of my actions that I would be safe, and it negated any temptation I might have to visit my children. My wife would have to decide if she would report me, and there was nothing I could do to lighten that burden. I could stay away, though, to not make it heavier.

It has been six years since I left home. I no longer work in psychiatry. I changed my name and started working from a distance for a technology firm. It is easy work and provides me with ample solitude. I do not try to build relationships anymore. I don't want them. I had worked in the industry before, so I was already equipped to do well.

All of my children should be in school now. I assume my wife has moved on and found a new partner. I don't check in on them much. My oldest daughter has a social media account. I found it a year ago when I randomly searched their names to ensure they weren't in any news articles. I committed to myself that I would only look at it once a year on her birthday. I get irritated that the privacy settings aren't more restrictive, but I also appreciate that I am able to see photos of her as she grows. I often wonder if her mother made the assumption that I might stumble upon it.

I make no attempts to see my wife. I doubt she has any interest in hearing from me, and I think it is appropriate to respect that much. She is raising my children without my presence, after all. I diligently monitored news reports for several months after I left. It seems like my wife never reported me to the police. I tried to understand her motivation at first, but I don't think I will ever have an answer. It could have been to protect the children, or to respect our time together, or because she knew that it was futile and they would never find me. Regardless, I left her with access to my bank accounts and chose only to survive with the money I brought and the money I earn here. There was enough in those accounts to keep them comfortable for a while.

I haven't stopped killing. I have refined my skills throughout the years and continue to work unnoticed by law enforcement. Thailand is extremely chaotic, which makes my work easy. I still do my best to ensure that I only target people I deem fitting, but without the constraints of a family, I can be more flexible with that rule.

Overall, I would say my life is comfortable and functional. I do miss my family at times, but I don't feel a great longing to see them. I miss them like I would miss my favorite painting. It was a part of my life for so long that I often notice its absence. I wish the best for them and would still do anything I could if they were ever in danger, but I realize now that they were my collar and my kennel. Initially, when I didn't have them, I felt like a domesticated dog that didn't know how to survive in the wild. Now, I might miss them, but I realize that I was never supposed to live life that way. It isn't in my nature.

When I'm not working or hunting, I have a plethora of time to reflect. That one question from my wife that I could never fully answer haunted my thoughts. I wanted to better understand myself, and so I had to look inward. Without my family, work relationships, and having to function around others, I was able to take a true and honest look at myself.

I realized that most people see the world and humanity from the same perspective. Do what is right and do what helps others. Yet it never matters to them if they are factually doing the most beneficial thing; it only matters that they think they are.

I tried to live like that for a long time. I tried to mask who I was to fit in, because that is what I was told I was supposed to do. I had a career, a house, a wife, and through the years even had some friends. I genuinely tried to be like everyone else. It didn't work for me. I don't see the world from the same angle. I grew tired of watching people filled with hate and entitlement and couldn't bring myself to "do what is best" for them.

I hated trying to feel the emotions that other people base their choices on. Love, guilt, compassion, happiness. It was always a confusing and frustrating process for me that only led to failed attempts to be different than I was.

I have stopped thinking about those urges as some kind of different version of me that I suppress when necessary. They are me. There is no dark self hiding away in the shadows. I simply prefer the shadows. I prefer to see the world from the other side.

I often revisit my past kills in my mind, but the one that my reflections have most often brought me back to is Gray, that pitiful stray from my childhood. I had no emotion, no empathy, no sympathy. I watched a creature I had developed a bond with die, and I couldn't have cared less.

I have discovered that I am often jealous of people that function well in society. They don't have to fake anything. They get the benefit of a village to support them and help them. I rebuilt my life, and at no point in the process did I even think about how others could help me. I only considered how much a relationship would hold me back in the process. I wish I was haunted by missing my children, but I can logically understand that my presence in their life wouldn't benefit me or them.

And as I have continued to ponder that one question, I've finally found my answer. Why wouldn't I do everything I did? There is nothing inherently wrong with me. I was never broken. So many years I wasted wondering if the right amount of purpose and connection could help heal me from an injury that I never sustained.

I wasn't meant to be a part of the world I was raised

in. I understand that now. I was just...passing through it. Mimicking its patterns, borrowing its language, forming my masks. Now, I no longer think about those things. I wake, I work, I hunt, I sleep. I watch the sun rise and set on each day, able to be a truer version of myself.

I never needed to change. And I will no longer pretend I ever will.

NOTE FROM THE AUTHOR

This story began as my own reflection on different concepts, such as morality, justice, or love, and how other people might view them differently. Before I knew it, I had transitioned the writing to the fictional memoir of someone who views his own actions as detached from what society expects as possible. I wanted to explore the difference between what we see in people and what they see in themselves.

If you have made it to the end, thank you. Thank you for your curiosity, your patience, and your willingness to explore the darker parts of the human mind.

JC MOWREY served in the military before becoming a licensed mental health professional with experience working with personality disorders. He enjoys writing horror and psychological fiction that is designed to challenge how people see humanity and right versus wrong.

facebook.com/jcmowreybooks
instagram.com/jc.mowrey

www.ingramcontent.com/pod-product-compliance
Lightning Source LLC
Chambersburg PA
CBHW030652260626
47157CB00007B/2609